Body Snatched

by

Ana Diamond

Body Conscious Series

Body Snatched

Cover Art by *Kristian Norris*

The Wild Rose Press, Inc.
PO Box 708
Adams Basin, NY 14410-0708
Visit us at www.thewildrosepress.com

Publishing History
First Edition, 2022
Trade Paperback ISBN 978-1-5092-4555-0
Digital ISBN 978-1-5092-4556-7

Body Conscious Series
Published in the United States of America

Black River reminded James of one thing: murder.

Hidden in dense foliage, the river stretched out far beyond his view and also happened to be a perfect spot to dump a body. He had no doubt there had been many missing people over the years who wound up weighed down by rocks at the bottom of the river until their flesh disintegrated into nothing.

His boss, Donald Abrams had a bad habit of telling him about their worst cases, probably to freak him out. The sicko with the garden of people floating upright like weeds was particularly gruesome. The chills he got from that one made the hairs on his neck stand up. However, since Manorview's crime rate was low, James wasn't entirely sure if the stories were folklore or not.

"Congrats on your last case. I heard you're a big boss detective now," Rick said as he reeled in his empty line.

James impaled a worm on his hook and swung the line out into the water. "Thanks. I wouldn't say big boss though. More like maybe I'll get to keep my job."

"Have you ever caught anything here?" Rick asked.

"No, but I hear there's trout."

And bodies.

Praise for Ana Diamond

Chapter One

"What do you mean it's gone?"

Stunned, Lily Reynolds sat at her desk on the first floor of the Reynolds Funeral Home and stared at her sister. "Zachary texted me as soon as he inserted it into the refrigerator. It didn't get up and walk away."

Shanna's eyebrows shot up. "It didn't walk away on its own, but it's definitely gone."

Lily stood. "Show me. I need to see for myself."

Both sisters barreled down the funeral home's stairs all the way to the basement level where the newly acquired *clients* were kept. When they reached the refrigerators, Lily noticed the third door from the bottom had not been fully closed.

"You left the door open?" Lily asked.

"I looked inside and saw that the body was gone," Shanna said. "It could've been stolen. I wanted to preserve the scene."

"Who'd steal a body?" Lily craned her neck to look inside the refrigerator. *Empty.*

"Someone clearly unwell."

"Does the family know?" Lily asked.

"I haven't had time to tell anyone but you. We should call the cops."

Lily glared at her sister.

"I know you're doing the detective thing on the side but you need help with this one."

1

Lily allowed an obnoxious eye roll to do the talking.

"The goal shouldn't be to prove to your new detective husband that you're as good as he is—we know that already," Shanna lectured.

"I'm not trying to prove anything, but I also don't want to call him every time we have an issue."

"I would call this more than an *issue*. Did Zachary go out again?"

"I'm about to." Their younger brother Zachary skipped down the stairs, heading in their direction. "What's all the chatter about?"

"You can't leave," Shanna told him. "We have a problem."

Lily gestured toward the open compartment. "*This* is the problem."

Unlike his sisters, Zachary didn't need to stand on his toes to see inside. He cocked his head at the empty tray. "Where's Mr. Gusev? I just dropped him off."

"You have no idea what happened to him?" Lily asked.

"I slid him in on the tray and even remembered to close the chamber door. Did one of you bring him upstairs and forget?"

"No," Shanna explained. "I came down to check on him as I always do when we get a new client and found this door open with no one inside."

"Where could he have gone?" Lily asked. "Was the family on board with moving him from the hospital after he was pronounced dead?"

"Completely," Zachary replied. "All the paperwork was signed."

Shanna pulled her cell phone from her pocket. "I'm calling the cops."

"Fine," Lily barked. "At least it's not me dialing the numbers. They'll be expecting you."

Shanna stuck her tongue out at her.

****

Despite her initial reluctance, Lily's mood brightened when Detective James Rivers showed up at the scene a short time later. She'd never get enough of his sun-kissed-tattooed biceps, pushing against the fabric of his rolled-up shirt sleeves and the brightness of his sky-blue eyes framed by silken black hair. The sight of him made her loins ache. How had she gotten so lucky?

He leaned in to peck her on the lips. "Mrs. Rivers, this is rather unexpected—getting a call from you for help on a case."

His stare made her knees weak; the same went for her conviction. She looked away, hoping that would help. "I didn't call you." She pointed a finger in her sister's direction. "She did."

He turned to Shanna. "What can I do for you?"

Lily looked at her sister, waiting for her to respond. After all, *she* wanted to call him. As much as Lily liked seeing her husband, she did not need his help with this.

"It appears that one of our clients is missing," Shanna said.

He glanced at Lily. "You lost a body?"

Her shoulders went up immediately. "We didn't *lose* a body. That's ridiculous. It's just...missing."

"Someone stole it," Zachary announced from his spot against the wall.

"Is that your theory?" James asked.

Zachary's hands went up. "It's the only thing that makes sense."

James cocked his head. "Stealing a body makes

sense to you?"

"It makes more sense than misplacing one. Plus, I don't like how you're judging us, Detective."

James smiled. "I'm not judging. I'm trying to make sure the body hasn't been relocated on the premises before we go barking up the stolen tree."

"Well, it's not here." Zachary answered quickly.

James approached the empty storage compartment. "Who was the first to notice the body had gone missing?"

Shanna's hand went up as if she were sitting in a classroom. "Me."

"You found the door open?"

"Yes, I left it the way I found it, in case there are fingerprints."

"Good thinking."

"Shouldn't you call the team over to secure the scene?" Lily asked, arms crossed over her chest. "We're pumping refrigerated air in here."

James scrutinized her for a second. She knew her attitude sucked. She didn't like it when they worked together; he stepped on her toes. After all, she wasn't a real detective. Technically anyway.

"Would you like to take over?" James asked. "I'm only trying to help."

Zachary and Shanna had slowly inched away. Lily saw their discomfort. Only married a month, she and James were still in the honeymoon period, yet she pushed him away. Her behavior could only be described as ridiculous. The man of her dreams stood in front of her and all she could manage was a pout.

"I know you're trying to help. I'm being unreasonable. I know. It'd be nice if Shanna wouldn't jump the gun by calling you. I'd like to think that I have good instincts even if I don't officially work for the police department."

James tilted his head. "Maybe you should."

Lily scanned his face carefully. Was he saying what she thought he was saying? "Can we do that?"

He snatched up her hands from their position on her waist. "We can try."

She hadn't expected to smile much today given the unpleasant set of circumstances but leave it to James to turn it all around. "Do we ask the boss, Detective Abrams?"

"His relationship with Shanna helps your cause, and he's my superior so we have to ask him. I'm not too worried about convincing him." He brought her hand up to kiss it gently. "It's you I'm worried about."

"I know. I know. Dangerous situations, blah, blah, blah." His toothy smile stopped her heart. "But I think it's the right move. I won't be happy waiting around for you to save the day. Don't get me wrong, I want to work together but I need some authority. I can't ride your coattails forever."

He pulled her toward him. "But I want you to ride my coattails."

She put her arms around his neck as he leaned down to press his lips against hers. Electric shocks pulsed through her body. It never got old. He had a way of turning her into jelly with one look.

"Are we good?" he asked.

How could she be anything but good? "We're more than good."

"I think we've scared away the rest of your family. Shall we call over some investigators to get this case rolling?"

"Sounds good, Detective."

His eyes twinkled. "So you lost a body."

Lily glared at him. It was bad enough a client had gone missing. She hated looking incompetent in front of her hot detective husband.

"And how do you know the body wasn't cremated by someone?"

"We would know if the ovens were being used by someone else. Plus, it's not an easy thing to hide as it takes several hours to cremate a body."

"All right, someone stole it. Why?"

She shrugged. "Could be an argument between the various family members."

James took out a small flashlight to see the dark crevices behind the appliances. "Have you seen that before?"

"Once—a disagreement among the relatives. Usually we make sure everyone is onboard with the final arrangements, but Mrs. Fisher was taken right out of the embalming room."

"How do you know it was a disagreement? What if they had plans to steal other bodies, including Mr. Gusev?"

"They left a note apologizing for their change of plan and they still paid the bill in full."

James's face scrunched into a look of confusion. "What did they do with it?"

"Hell if I know." Lily shrugged. "The death had already been reported to the state. The note mentioned something about burying the body near a cousin. I hope they didn't keep it in their back bedroom."

James flashed his light in her direction. "Tell me why you do this job again?"

"To keep Manorview PD busy."

He pursed his lips. "Funny."

"If it's not a family member, then what are we left with? Some sicko interested in bodies?"

"Anything is possible. We'll have to start with anyone close to you and the rest of your family. If you can pull your client list, we can start looking for any connections."

"Could be random, I suppose."

"Could be," he said, continuing to check out the scene of the *crime,* "but I didn't notice any forced entry when I got here. How would they have gotten in here?"

"So you're saying it's an inside job?"

He gave her one of his patented looks of husbandly patience. "I'm not saying anything. Yet. I'm calling the team over to take a look and collect evidence. Maybe there are fingerprints we can use. Who knows? We may have an expert lockpicker on our hands."

"Sounds good. I'm going to make sure Chris and Marcia are here and know that we've hit a small snafu."

"How has Chris Tuchman been doing as your new manager?"

"I have no complaints."

"And Marcia Alonso? Are her makeover skills as good as yours?" With a wink, he waggled his brows. "Nobody brings a body back to life like you."

"True. But she'll have to fill in for me if I'm going to solve this case."

James clenched his jaw. "We'll see about that."

"Hello!" A booming male voice could be heard from the main floor upstairs. "Anybody home?"

Lily's eyes went wide. "Who's that?" she asked in a whisper.

"We're down here in the basement," James announced then glanced in Lily's direction. "My old buddy, Rick Drakon, from The City. We worked together in the Bronx before I moved up here. He'd been staying at Riverside Bed and Breakfast, but I told him he could stay with us for a bit."

"Here? At the funeral home?"

"Just for a few days."

The steps leading from above stretched and groaned as a massive male frame bounded down the stairs.

"Hey, buddy," James said and leaned into the man for a guy hug.

"Long time, no see. Thanks for letting me stay."

Lily watched them embrace. The light from the fluorescent bulbs on the ceiling reflected off the man's shiny bald head.

"Lily, this Rick Drakon, an old friend," James said, and gave his pal a playful slap on the back. "Rick, this is my wife, Lily. I'm sorry you couldn't make it to the wedding."

"Work does get in the way sometimes. I should have called in sick." She smelled the aroma of musk cologne emanating from his black T-shirt. The gold chain hanging from his neck swayed as Rick leaned over, took her hand and planted a kiss on the top. "Enchanted."

"Nice to meet you, Rick." She didn't know what else to say. James had sprung this on her at the last minute. "Welcome to my funeral home."

She watched for his reaction. Not everyone wanted to sleep amongst the dead.

He grinned. "Thank you for having me."

She didn't detect any trepidation on his part and could respect that. "You can stay in my sister's old room.

She recently moved out and got a place of her own."

"I appreciate that. I promise I won't get in the way of business."

"I'll show him around town," James said. "Obviously, this is not a big town but there's some good fishing by Black River. We've got bass and pike."

Lily had a thought. "Actually, we could use your help. It'd be nice to get an outside perspective on a case we've…stumbled upon."

James gave her a disapproving look, but she didn't care. If she had more than one detective on hand, she wanted to use every available resource to help find the culprit. "The case won't solve itself," she told him.

"I'd love to help." Rick's eyes narrowed. "What seems to be the problem?"

Lily pointed to the open refrigerator compartment. "One of our bodies was snatched."

Chapter Two

Black River reminded James of one thing: murder.

Hidden in dense foliage, the river stretched out far beyond his view and also happened to be a perfect spot to dump a body. He had no doubt there had been many missing people over the years who wound up weighed down by rocks at the bottom of the river until their flesh disintegrated into nothing.

His boss, Donald Abrams had a bad habit of telling him about their worst cases, probably to freak him out. The sicko with the garden of people floating upright like weeds was particularly gruesome. The chills he got from that one made the hairs on his neck stand up. However, since Manorview's crime rate was low, James wasn't entirely sure if the stories were folklore or not.

"Congrats on your last case. I heard you're a big boss detective now," Rick said, as he reeled in his empty line.

James impaled a worm on his hook and swung the line out into the water. "Thanks. I wouldn't say big boss though. More like maybe I'll get to keep my job."

"Have you ever caught anything here?"

"No, but I hear there's trout."

And bodies.

"A fat trout would be nice to bring home for dinner."

James swallowed, imagining bodies suspended over the river bottom. "It sure would."

"And Lily helps with your cases?"

"Yes, after we discovered she had a talent for it. I'm not thrilled about it though."

"I bet. After what happened to Andrea, I'm sure your work is the last thing you want Lily involved in."

James pressed his lips together. Tight. The death of his previous girlfriend had been his fault. He allowed her to be in the wrong place at the wrong time in crossfire and she was killed. Not only did he have to live with himself for not being able to protect her, but he'd been letting Lily creep dangerously close to that line as well. He hadn't slept well in a long time.

"You're right, I don't want Lily involved but I'm not sure I can stop her either."

"I'd like to help with your case but without fingerprints it's not going to be easy."

James sucked in a breath. "I know. The forensics report didn't help much. I was hoping there would be some prints somewhere but no such luck. Whoever did it knew what they were doing."

"No other clues?"

"None. Lily will talk to the family. That won't be easy." James felt a few wet raindrops slide down his neck as he reeled in his line. The worm had vanished.

"Are they biting them off yours too?"

"I stopped trying. I don't think there's any fish in there. How 'bout a brew?" Rick tossed a can of beer to James.

"Sounds good—starting to rain anyway." James dropped his fishing pole and hooked his finger under the pull-tab. He snapped it forward, letting the gas escape.

Rick took a long swig of his beer. Then wiped his mouth with the back of his meaty hand. He put his baseball cap on and sat on top of the cooler they'd brought. "But seriously, how are things?"

"Good. Quite a change from the big city but that's what I wanted. And then I met Lily."

"I tell you, I wasn't expecting you to meet someone so fast. I thought if either of us was going to meet someone it would be me."

James wiped away the moisture from his eyebrow. "I'm better looking."

"Maybe. But I'm a better detective and by default my checkered past makes me more interesting than you," Rick said, taking another swig.

"You don't have a checkered past. We have no control over who raises us. So your family made some mistakes. You're the total opposite. You're in law enforcement."

"But you know what they say."

"What's that?"

"The apple doesn't fall far from the tree."

James laughed. "I don't have time to investigate you. I'm too busy dropping worms into the river. Plus, who's going to watch over things here when Lily and I go on our honeymoon?"

"Does she know?"

"No, it's a surprise and you better not tell her."

All kidding left Rick's face. "But does she *know*?"

James watched his buddy's dark eyes. He knew what Rick referred to but decided to play dumb. Rick knew all about his past and having him enter into his new life meant opening up old wounds.

He gulped down some beer. "Does she know what?"

Rick's eyebrows shot up. "Does she know about *everything*?"

James looked toward the large raindrops breaking through the river's surface ahead. The silvery-green water reminded him of Lily's eyes and how he'd crumble if he lost her. "No, I haven't told her."

"Don't you think she has a right to know since you're married now?"

"She has the right but I'm afraid once she finds out all the things I did to comfort myself after Andrea's death she'll leave me. The drugs, alcohol, and total self-destruction. I don't want her to think she's married to the wrong guy."

"It was a long time ago, buddy. But I wouldn't blame her if she was upset that you didn't tell her *before* she decided to marry you."

James stared at the muddy puddles starting to form by his feet. "Will you do me a solid and tell her for me?"

Rick shook his head. "I'm the single one, remember? You don't want me doing the dirty work." He walked over to James and slapped him on the back. "If she loves you, she'll understand. We all have a past. I bet she has one, too."

"She does—a dark one. But mine is full of mistakes I made. There's a difference."

"Geez." Rick pointed toward the river. "Don't jump in. I don't want to have to go in after you and get my leather jacket even more soaked."

"No, you're right. I should've told her. But I don't want her to think I'll ever go down that road again."

"Will you?"

James watched drops dangle for a second. The question scared him. What would drive him to the path of self-destruction again? He knew the answer—losing Lily. And would she leave if she found out he'd been withholding the ugly side of him? He shuddered. She might. "Will I ever go down that dark path again? I don't know."

****

"I'm so sorry this happened." Lily said to the frowning woman. "I assure you, we've never experienced anything like this in the fifty years we've been in business."

"And yet it happened. Klaus deserves better than this. He worked hard all his life in that no-good factory for thirty-five years. The least we could do is give him a peaceful afterlife." She pushed a tissue under her eye to catch her tears.

"I promise we will do everything we can to find Klaus and give him the burial you wanted, Mrs. Gusev. Free of charge."

Her eyes perked up a bit. She began dotting the wetness from her other cheek. "That's generous of you. Have the police found anything?"

"They are working very hard on this case. As part of the investigational team I want you to know I will do anything in my power to find Klaus."

The corner of her mouth lifted. "You're a cop?"

"Well, sort of. I've been recruited to help solve these types of crimes but I'm not officially on their payroll *yet*. I guarantee I am as good as their best detective. Maybe even better."

Mrs. Gusev's right eyebrow rose. "If you are part of the investigation, then what have you found?"

"Honestly, not much. No fingerprints were left at the scene. No items were left behind that could identify our thief. But we're still looking and part of that means asking for your help as well."

14

"Call me Katia. What can I do to help?"

Phew.

Lily's shoulders relaxed a bit. She had succeeded in pacifying her client and convinced the grieving woman she could be as helpful as any cop. "Do you think there is anyone out there who may wish Klaus harm? Maybe they'd been planning some kind of revenge after he passed?"

Katia's gray eyes focused on the ground. "Klaus was a good husband as far as I can tell but he didn't tell me everything. He ran with a few characters."

"Would those characters ever break the law?"

"I can't say for sure. There are a couple I think should be questioned." She leaned forward. "As long as you don't mention my name. I run in close circles. I don't want to be ousted by my own group."

"Understood. Your identity won't be revealed."

"Do you have a pen and paper?"

"Certainly." Lily opened the drawer on the left side of her desk. She pulled out a notepad and handed Katia a pen.

She watched Katia hesitate on producing the names. This seemed like a lead Lily could sink her teeth into. Thoughts popped around her mind like popcorn. Maybe there was a group of outsiders who she could put the squeeze on to talk about the crime. Maybe Klaus had some enemies looking to humiliate him. She had read his death certificate. It had been ruled a death from natural causes but who knows? All Katia had to do was write a list of names and the flood gates could swing wide open right before her very eyes.

"This is strictly confidential," Lily added. "Your identity will never be revealed to those people."

Mrs. Gusev offered Lily a crooked smile. "They'll know I said something. The question is, do I care?"

"If it leads to an arrest and finding Klaus, then it's worth the risk. We can offer you protection." Lily assumed that was the case. She'd make sure James authorized it.

Katia began scribbling on the notepad. After, she stared at Lily with her hand posed over what she'd written. "I hope you're right." She removed her hand and slid the notepad to Lily.

"You have done a good thing. We'll look into this and get back to you if we find anything."

Katia's eyes teared up again. "Please find Klaus."

"I will. I promise. Thank you for your cooperation."

Katia gathered her purse and grabbed another tissue from the box on the desk as she stood.

Lily walked her to the front door. "As soon as I hear something I will call you," she told her.

"Thank you," Katia said as she walked to her car.

Lily watched her get into the car as if checking to make sure she was well enough to drive. She couldn't believe this terrible mess. If she were in Katia's shoes, would she be as reasonable? Probably not.

"Is that the wife?"

Lily jumped. Rick had snuck up behind her. "Yes." She closed the front door with force. Even though he'd been staying in Shanna's room, Lily hadn't quite gotten used to the idea of having him around.

"Is she pissed?" he asked.

"Wouldn't you be?"

"Yes, but you never know. Maybe she did it."

"Katia? No. I haven't been investigating for very long, but I know my clients. She didn't do it. She may know who did though."

Rick pursed his lips and chuckled. "Sounds like you have a lead. Although, you know how those go. You think you've got a lead and then it turns out to be something else altogether."

Lily examined her husband's friend from his shiny scalp to his combat boots. *Who is this guy?*

"Does that happen to you often in the field?"

He shrugged. "It happens. Katia is probably emotional right now. All she wanted to do was bury her husband in a reputable funeral home and the guy gets kidnapped? How often does that happen?"

Lily cocked her head. "Not often but thanks for the recap."

"It reminds me of a cold case I had a few years back in The City. A hospital worker wheeled several deceased bodies out of the hospital on their stretchers. No one ever saw the dead people again."

Lily's eyebrows shot up. "That's crazy. What were they doing? Selling organs?"

"Probably. Maybe. I had no idea. We never found any of them."

"Are you saying the thief might work here and I should look within the company?"

"I'm not saying that." He shook his head. "I'm saying that case dragged on forever."

"So you never caught whoever did it?"

"No, the case went cold. For years I chased it and never got anywhere. I was so frustrated at how often I would chase leads that would never pan out. I almost walked out on law enforcement. It drove me mad."

Lily stared at his dark eyes. "That's not very encouraging."

He put his hands up in surrender. "Just saying."

She barely knew him but something about him seemed off. He seemed to be putting her off the case. But why? Was he confused by her participation in the case? If so, he had another thing coming.

"I'll take my chances. Katia deserves to know what happened."

He bowed his head and walked back up to Shanna's bedroom.

Her eyes narrowed as she studied him. She couldn't quite put her finger on it. But she couldn't shake the feeling that there was more than meets the eye with Rick. And she had to trust her instincts.

They hadn't led her astray…yet.

Chapter Three

Lily stared at the names Katia had provided. Then she looked at James as he sat at his desk on the other side of the room. He cradled the phone receiver on one shoulder while taking notes with the opposite hand, He had other cases to deal with. This one was hers.

Vlad Petrov. The first name on the list.

Nerves made her palms sweaty. It's not like she had a vast amount of experience to fall back on, but she couldn't help the enormous pressure to succeed. If Vlad had stolen Klaus's body, she may already be close to solving the case and clearing the criminal stain on her business.

She dialed the number Katia had provided.

"Hello?" A deep raspy voice answered on the first ring.

"Is this Vlad Petrov?"

"Yes."

"My name is Lily Reynolds. I wanted to ask you some questions about Klaus Gusev."

"What kind of questions? Are you a cop?"

Lily struggled with this type of question. She wanted to say, "of course." But that would be a bold-faced lie. Plus, he'd probably hang up if she confirmed it.

"No, Mr. Petrov, I own Reynolds Funeral Home. Klaus Gusev's body was entrusted to us but has gone missing. This is now considered a crime and under police investigation. I thought you might know something that might be helpful to them."

"His dead body went missing? That's terrible. What kind of a place are you running over there? Katia must be beside herself."

Lily blinked a few times. It sounded crazy hearing it over and over. Her funeral home *lost* a body. Although hard to hear, Vlad was right. It was a terrible tragedy.

"It was stolen from our facility. We are devastated by the incident and want to do everything we can to fix the issue. That's why I'm calling, to see if you have any information or a lead we can follow." Silence followed, long enough for Lily to fear the line had gone dead. "Hello? Mr. Petrov?"

He cleared his throat. "That could only be an inside job. Maybe someone on your staff sold it for some extra bucks. I read that in the news once. A couple of years ago a group of embalmers got together and started selling organs. Until the day a package containing two kidneys wound up lost in the mail. The cold packs started melting in the summer heat and the smell prompted the mail service to open the box. That ended their enterprise."

"Our funeral home is family-run." Although not entirely true since they hired Chris and Marcia. Plus, Antonio has been their hearse driver for years—close enough to consider him family. "No one is selling organs. I think maybe someone wanted revenge on Klaus. Would you know anything about that?"

"Let me tell you something. Everyone who knew Klaus loved him. He used to babysit my daughter's kids. There wasn't a bad bone in that man's body. You won't find a hater anywhere in sight. When he passed away from the heart attack, the whole neighborhood came out to pay respects to Katia."

"Understood. But that doesn't mean—"

"It means you're barking up the wrong tree. Klaus was a good friend and I hate that this happened to him. I suggest you figure out why you're losing bodies over there before your reputation makes your business go belly up."

The silence on the other end meant Vlad had hung up on her. She reclined in her chair and let out a breath. This didn't feel right. She wanted the phone call to be the break into the case but all she'd manage to do was make her business look bad. She clicked the top of her pen repeatedly. This detecting stuff was harder than she'd anticipated.

"Are you all right over there?" James asked, startling her out of her thoughts.

She never could hide her feelings. "Not really."

He stood up and walked over to her desk. "Need help? Or am I not allowed?"

She stood up and breathed in his musky scent. No matter how long they've been together his scent always drew her in and disarmed her. "I think my lead just blew up in my face."

He looked down at her list. "Are you sure?"

"Pretty sure. Seemed too easy anyway."

He put his arm around her waist. "Don't give up. Sometimes you need to walk away and pursue something else then come back to it. Did you call both of them?"

She wanted to forget the whole thing and smooch. "No, there's no point."

"It happens all the time. Don't give up."

"I won't give up but I'm a little depressed—not going to lie."

"Maybe this will help." He leaned toward her, planting his soft lips on hers.

Her belly ignited. It did help. He pulled away before things could go further. "I'll never get anything done."

"That's *your* problem. You gave me the desk."

"True. But I have no regrets."

She narrowed her eyes. "Now that our house is full of guests this might actually be the best place for some flirting."

He returned a crooked smile. "I was wondering when you were going to bring that up. Rick is only staying for a few days. He's not going to ruin our lives."

"I know that, but you sprung it up on me. I'm not the best with surprises."

"Fair enough. Ask me anything. He's an old friend and he's a pretty good detective. He's single. Maybe Shanna would like him."

"Oh, stop. You know she's all about Don Abrams. When she told me she was going to move in with him I didn't believe it. Stop trying to sabotage them."

"Abrams deserves a good kick in the balls. It would make him feel a little insecure—might do him some good."

"Shanna's my sister and I guess she loves him. Leave them alone. Plus, Rick is not her type."

"Big, burly, and bald?"

"No. Though that's quite the opposite of Abrams."

"Rick's a good guy. I think you need to give him a chance. Let's all have a nice dinner tonight. You two can get to know each other and then maybe you'll understand why I call him my buddy."

"Deal. What does he like to eat?"

"No idea."

"You two sound real close."

He returned one of his famous heart-stopping kilowatt smiles. "It'll be great. I promise."

****

Lily watched Rick scoop another heaping spoonful of Shanna's lasagna onto his plate. She took credit for it making it—not wanting him to think she couldn't cook. The truth was, she liked to prepare meals, but not when her business managed to lose a body and she had to figure out who did it before anyone else reported her to the state. Nope, right now cooking was not a priority.

"How are you getting along with the folks at Manorview PD?" Lily asked. "I'd imagine it's quite different from the NYPD."

"It is different but in a good way. The people are nicer. I went to the Coffee Cup this morning and had a conversation with the owner, Riley, about the perks of slowing down the pace."

"And?" she asked.

"It's pleasant, a nice change."

"I'm glad you're enjoying your stay. I, in turn, had to speak with Katia, the wife of the man whose body was stolen, allegedly."

"That's not as fun. How's the case coming along?" Rick asked in between chews.

Lily glanced at James. He returned a deep sigh.

"That well?" Rick asked.

"I thought I had a good lead but I'm not sure anymore. I might be back to square one," she answered.

"It happens all the time," Rick said, stabbing his fork into bites of pasta and popping them into his mouth.

Lily pushed food around her plate. "Still, it doesn't feel good."

"No, but it is part of the process. Haven't you taught her that yet, James? Or are you so perfect it never happens to you?"

"I don't get involved unless she wants me to be. I learned that a long time ago."

"That's a good point. Being single, I'm not familiar with that angle."

"Are you single because of the job?" Lily asked.

"Lily!" James scolded her.

Rick smiled. "No, it's fine. I guess you could say I haven't found the right person yet. And that is largely due to the job. The late nights, being constantly on-call and the inconvenient possibility of death at any moment. I'd say I'm not that popular."

"That sounds familiar. If you're ever thinking about moving out of The City, I'm sure I have a few girlfriends who'd take a chance on you."

"That's nice of you. Eventually, I would like a family. I might need to transition to a desk job of some sort before that happens. My last relationship ended because at the time I was working nights and sleeping most of the day. She couldn't envision herself living that way. I thought I needed someone more understanding, so we broke up."

"Sorry to hear that," Lily said, slicing through the layers of pasta. "How long have you known James?"

"Long enough to know he's a great detective and person."

"Aww." Lily watched James smirk, but he kept his eyes on his plate. "You don't have to be embarrassed. It's all true."

"You're just saying that, Rick, because you want to win her over," James said.

"You never know. I might decide I like Manorview so much I end up moving here."

"You should." James said. "I for one love all the rumors and small-town gossip."

"It's not that bad." Lily smacked his shoulder. "It's quite nice actually. But it would be a change of pace for you, Rick."

"You never know. Clearly, I would need your help meeting people." Rick pointed at Lily.

"A charming guy like yourself wouldn't need too much help, maybe just an introduction. I'd be more than happy to help but only after you tell me who took Mr. Klaus Gusev."

A flash of something in his dark brown eyes made Lily pause.

Then he resumed his cheerful vibe. "I'm at your service but without any hard evidence you might need to cut your losses."

"I'll circle back and make sure I haven't missed anything."

She half-smiled. But her mind was no longer on trying to make friends. She had her initial doubts about Rick and had swept them aside to appease James but now there was no mistake about it. The air in the room had shifted.

And Rick Drakon was hiding something.

Chapter Four

At the station, James closed the file on his desk, then stretched his arms out with a yawn. *Finally done.*

The station had been nice and quiet for most of the day, giving him the opportunity to sink his teeth into the mountainous pile on his desk. Even if it had only been one of many files, he was happy to have finished the paperwork on his burglary case. It hadn't been his toughest challenge, but it hadn't been a walk in the park either. If the victim had a less questionable background, he would've had an easier time on the stand. Regardless, the case was closed, and he wasn't sad about it.

He glanced over at Lily's empty desk. Typically during the week, she spent some days at the funeral home and other days here working on cases. She'd told him she wanted to catch up with work at the funeral home today. He thought that had been odd. She always wanted to be here, cranking away at each case. But he suspected she didn't want to be here today because she had hit a roadblock on the Klaus Gusev case.

James sniffed. He promised he would stay out of her way so she wouldn't feel like he was being overprotective. But he couldn't resist the urge to help her whenever possible. He stood up and walked over to her desk. She'd left a manila folder in the center of the table. He flipped it open to find two names on a list.

Vlad Petrov and Demetri Popov.

He remembered she had abandoned the lead after the first phone call, although he couldn't be certain she didn't call the second person on the list. Grabbing the list off her desk, he decided he would take the risk she might get upset if it meant pushing the case further. Besides, a missing body in a funeral home was bad for business. This case had to get solved sooner rather than later.

James returned to his desk and dialed the second phone number on the list.

"Hello?" A deep voice answered.

"Mr. Popov?"

"Yes, who's calling?"

"This is detective James Rivers from Manorview PD. I am investigating the disappearance of Klaus Gusev's body. Would you mind answering some questions?"

A long pause on the other end made James think this would not go in his favor.

"As a matter of fact, I'm glad you called. I have some information you might be interested in. I think you should come meet me. I've got something to show you."

James's heart thumped—not what he had expected. "Sure, I can meet you if you think it's worthwhile."

"I think you'd be very interested."

James sucked in a breath. He didn't know what to think. Most civilians wanted nothing to do with him. It'd be better for him to meet up with this guy than Lily. "When and where?" he asked.

"This is very sensitive information I am providing you. I don't want anyone I know to see me with you near my house." Demetri chuckled. "Let's meet at Al's Diner in one hour. No one I know would eat in that place."

James glanced at the clock on his cell phone. Four

thirty. He could meet Demetri Popov and be back before Lily noticed he'd been gone. Since he knew Lily wanted to take the lead on the case the last thing he wanted to do was step on her toes. "I'll meet you at Al's in one hour," he told Popov. "Come alone and don't tell anyone we are meeting."

"You won't regret it."

"We'll see about that. Bye."

James hung up the phone with zero confidence that this was a legitimate lead. This guy Demetri was probably planning on getting his whole crew together to jump James for even trying to question him. He took his car keys out of his pants pocket and found the smallest key to open his locked desk drawer. Inside he took out his gun and ammunition. Loading the gun to full capacity, he wanted to make sure he was ready for anything.

"Making sure you still know how to load a gun?" Abrams said, poking his head into the office.

James didn't look up at him as he finished pushing the bullets into the cartridge. "I'm going to Al's to meet an acquaintance of the wife of the guy whose body was snatched from the Reynolds Funeral Home. He claims to know something about it."

Abrams shook his head. "Never dull at the Reynolds place. You need backup?"

"Probably. But at least I've told you where I'll be. I'm sure it'll be fine."

"Famous last words. I'll send a car over just in case."

"Whatever you say, boss." James got up, put his gun in his shoulder holster and walked toward Abrams. "Just don't tell Lily. This is her case."

"Right." Abrams put his hands up. "I know nothing about it, nor do I want to," he said as he walked toward his office. "Call if you need anything."

"Sure thing. Should be fine."

"I bet," Abrams said without looking back. "Should be fine."

****

Al's Diner usually had a substantial dinner crowd, but Monday nights were typically slow. After James parked his car in the lot next to the diner, he took a look at his surroundings. The patrol car Abrams sent sat in plain sight across the street—not the best choice. He hoped that wouldn't scare off Demetri. He also hoped he wouldn't run into a car full of big dudes with baseball bats waiting for him around the corner.

James stepped into the diner with laser focus. A mixed bag of kitchen smells ranging from burnt toast to hamburger grease filled his nostrils as his eyes swept the room for anything out of the ordinary and for his potential suspect.

A boisterous bunch of teens had gathered in a corner booth on one end while an older couple sat sipping soup across from each other at the other end of the restaurant. He took a few more steps inside when he noticed a thin elderly man stand up in his booth and wave James over. James hesitated at first, unclear what to expect but knew he couldn't back out now.

"Detective. I'm Demetri. Please have a seat."

James instantly felt relieved. At least he could rule out a total ambush. "How did you know who I was?"

"You have that look to you. Official, yet rough on the edges."

James didn't have a response.

The waiter approached their table. "Good evening, Frank. How are things?" James asked the long-time server.

Frank pushed his glasses farther up the bridge of his nose. "Not bad. Slow night."

"That's what you always say. I think you're just really efficient at what you do."

"I won't argue with you. And you're always working."

"True. But don't tell my wife."

Frank smiled. "What can I get you?"

"Nothing for me." James pointed at Demetri. "Mr. Popov?"

"Black tea for me."

"Right away." Frank walked away.

James cleared his throat and focused on the task at hand. "You have something to show me?"

"I don't like to beat around the bush. I haven't told Katia anything about this. I didn't want to upset her."

"She might know a little. She was the one who gave us your name."

Demetri rubbed the four o'clock shadow on his chin. "She meant no harm in it. She probably had a hunch I might know something."

"Or maybe *you* had something to do with the disappearance of the body."

Demetri pointed one finger up. "Once I explain, you'll understand."

Frank came back with Demetri's tea and placed it in front of him.

"Thank you." He took a sip as Frank walked away.

"I'm ready when you are," James told Popov.

Demetri placed the teacup in its dish and reached in

his back pocket. He slid a folded paper in front of James. It was folded in half like a brochure or flyer. The front page said *Zeus* centered in typed letters. The rest of the page was blank. James glanced at Demetri as he looked inside the brochure. There was a hasty sketch of a large house surrounded by woods with the number twelve written beneath it. He flipped the brochure over. The back had nothing written on it. He'd never seen anything so incredibly unhelpful.

James shrugged as he held the brochure with disinterest. "What does it mean?"

"It's a secret meeting—a group run by a guy who calls himself Zeus. They meet in the woods in a secluded area to practice rituals."

James looked at the drawing inside, frowning the entire time. "What does the twelve mean?"

"That I don't know. It might be a way they're communicating with each other—a code."

"So far, I've seen nothing illegal here. What's the connection?"

Demetri leaned forward a bit. His glossy blue eyes stared at James. "I have no proof, but I think this guy Zeus took Klaus."

James frowned. "Why would *Zeus* do that?"

Demetri's eyes went wide. "I think they used Klaus as a sacrifice—a human sacrifice."

James leaned back in the booth. This had not gone in the direction he'd anticipated. He held up the brochure. "Where did you get this?"

"It was handed to me near my church on Tremont Road. I go there for evening mass."

"Saint Nicholas Church?"

"Yes."

"Did you know the person who handed it to you?"

"No, I didn't know him, regular looking guy. But it was dark at that time and hard to see anything distinguishing about him."

"Have you been to one of their meetings?"

"Nah." Demetri grimaced. "That'd be a sacrilege. But the guy who handed it to me said his name was Sam. He told me if I wanted to follow a real leader I should go to the meetings."

"A real leader?"

"He said they meet to practice religion the ancient pure way, uncorrupted by modern life."

"Did he mention human sacrifice?"

"No, that's my interpretation."

James frowned. "How did you jump to that conclusion? Some random guy is helping recruit to a different church and suddenly there's human sacrifice?"

Demetri took another sip of his tea. "After Sam handed me the pamphlet I went to my church and asked if anyone had heard of such a meeting. You could say these were largely rumors but I trust my fellow churchgoers. They are good people."

"Your church friends suggested to you that there are rituals in the woods with human sacrifice, but you believe the human sacrifices are actually performed with bodies stolen from funeral homes?"

"Not just me. It is also believed to be true among my colleagues."

"And you don't know who Sam is?"

"No." Demetri smiled. "I know how this sounds but I wouldn't have wanted to meet if I didn't think this was all credible. All I'm asking is that you look into it. For Klaus."

The whole thing made James think he'd wasted half his day. He was certainly no historian, but human sacrifice typically happened with live bodies, not refrigerated ones waiting to be embalmed.

James felt his pants pocket vibrate. "Is there anything else you wanted to share?"

"No, that's about it."

"Thank you. If you'll excuse me for a minute, I'm going to take this call."

Demetri nodded and went back to sipping his tea.

James stood and walked out of the booth toward the diner entrance. "Hello?" He already had seen that the caller was Lily.

"You're not going to believe this." She sounded both alarmed and breathless. "It happened again."

"Believe what? What happened?"

"I had Shanna and Zachary double check in case I was losing my mind but they both agree that I'm not seeing things."

"That's comforting. Can you calm down and tell me what you saw before I send a police brigade down there?"

"You might as well send one, we're going to need it." Her voice came out muffled. It sounded like she was running around the funeral home.

"For what?" His voice came out stern and annoyed.

Her breathing slowed, as she seemed to finally stop her frenzied movement. "We're going to need help because another body was snatched."

Chapter Five

As soon as James rushed into her office, Lily burst into tears. He was the rock in her life and his presence unleashed raw emotions. "I don't understand. Who's doing this?"

All strong and comforting, he reached out to embrace her. "It's all right. We'll figure it out."

She buried her face in his shoulder. "Who in their right mind goes out of their way to take bodies out of a funeral home?" She wiped at her cheeks. "What are they doing with them? Those poor families. They've entrusted us with their loved ones, and we can't even keep them safe." Her arms flailed. Anger replaced the tears. "If I'd known there was a serial body snatcher, I would've hired a bodyguard to watch the place twenty-four hours a day."

"We can do that. We can have a patrol car stationed nearby." He rubbed her back from hips to the nape of her neck in long, firm strokes. "I didn't think it would happen again either. Doesn't make much sense. The only theory that's surfaced is completely ridiculous. We'll have to keep this place locked up tight and hope whoever is doing this comes around again for a third, and when he does, we'll snatch *him*."

Lily smiled. He had a way of making things better despite the obstacles. She sniffed and wiped away the remaining wetness from her cheeks. "What ridiculous theory came up?"

James sighed. "I don't want to make you more upset."

"Oh, great. It gets worse?"

"It's not bad. I was trying to help with this case."

She folded her arms across her chest. "Tell me."

"I saw the list on your desk and remembered you had abandoned the lead after the first call, so I rang the second guy on the list."

"Demetri Popov? You called my lead?" Her nostrils flared. "Without asking me?"

"I wanted to help. I didn't think it would go anywhere."

"And? Did it?"

"Demetri wanted to meet up and tell me who he thought was involved."

"Tell me you met up with him?" She leaned in closer to James.

One eyebrow rose. "Of course, I follow every lead."

Lily cocked her head. He was teasing, but she wasn't interested in playing.

Then he shook his head and smiled. "Don't worry. I didn't steal your case. It was a complete waste of time. He thinks there's a secret ancient religious group meeting in the woods somewhere practicing human sacrifice."

Lily frowned. "What?"

"I know it's completely insane. He showed me a flyer a six-year-old might have made." He pulled it out of his jacket pocket and placed it on her desk.

"Human sacrifice? As in murdering innocent people for religious purposes? Who are the victims?" She picked up the brochure. One look made her mouth drop open as her brain clicked into gear. "Are you saying this group is stealing my bodies for sacrifice?"

"It doesn't even make sense. Human sacrifice is with living people, not dead ones." His arms went out. "Isn't it?"

Lily scrunched up her face as she scrutinized the pamphlet. "I don't know. Did Demetri explain what all of this means?"

"He said the group is led by a guy who calls himself Zeus. The drawing of the house represents where they meet in the woods—not really clear on where that would be though."

Lily looked up from the brochure. "They would need a large local house with privacy. Whoever drew this also included a wooded area." She pointed to the tangled sketch of trees and bushes surrounding the house. "That's a helpful clue. And they also bothered to draw the stone blocks from which the house is constructed. My guess is the rituals are being conducted behind a very large house with a significant number of woods surrounding it, making the house more secluded than the average house in Manorview. That narrows the options down quite a bit."

"To how many?"

Lily raised her shoulders. "The first one that comes to my mind is the old Rubin mansion. It's been abandoned for years by that old doctor and his wife. They ran out of money building the place."

"Yeah, I know the story. Dr. George Rubin, the famous neurologist. He got pretty far with the building of that house before it got out of hand. One of the guys at the station told me the pool in the back has a large cave with a waterfall inside. Maybe that's what did him in."

"Maybe, but the old Rubin house is really secluded with a lot of woodlands behind it. I bet that's where this *Zeus* is holding his rituals."

"The whole thing sounds crazy to me," James said. "I think Demetri was handed this brochure by some looney tune. It's completely made up."

She pointed to the numbers. "What's the twelve mean?"

"No idea. Maybe it's a reference to the twelve days of Christmas."

Lily glared at him.

"Look, if you want to pursue Mr. Popov's brochure of terror, suit yourself. I'm here to investigate the theft of another body. Show me where it went missing from."

Lily placed the pamphlet on her desk. He was right about one thing. She had every intention of pursuing this lead. "The thief got a little more confident this time," she said as she led him out of her office.

"More confident?"

"The body was stolen out of here," she said, leading him into her make-up room.

"Are you sure?"

She cocked her head in response.

"It couldn't have been anywhere else?" he asked.

"You've been living here long enough to know what goes on here. There's a step-by-step process. I asked Zachary to help move Ms. Bernardo from the embalming room to this room for her make-up application."

"Where were you when this was going on?"

"In my office reviewing the family's specific make-up requests for her."

"How long were you in your office?"

"Twenty minutes."

"Then what?"

"I went into the make-up room, expecting to see Ms. Bernardo. I found the room empty. Then I checked the embalming room. She wasn't in there either."

"What did Zachary have to say about it?"

"He said he moved her in the make-up room and then he went back to restocking inventory."

"Is anyone else here?"

"Shanna was here earlier, embalming the same client but then she went out to dinner with Abrams after she finished."

"What about Antonio Reales? Is he out with the hearse?"

"He said he wanted to take it out to the car wash."

"What about Rick?"

"He made it a point to announce he needed to go run some errands."

"He took his truck?"

"I assume so." Lily shrugged her shoulders as she peered up the stairs at the door to Shanna's old bedroom. She suddenly got the urge to search the room.

"What about Chris and Marcia?" James asked.

"I sent Chris out to deposit checks at the bank. Marcia said she wanted to step out for some fresh air."

"Does she do that a lot?"

"Maybe. I haven't been keeping track of how often she has stepped out for fresh air."

"All right. I'll request the forensics team to come over. You never know if this person left a fingerprint or a strand of hair somewhere."

"If they have hair on their head," Lily mumbled.

"What?"

"Nothing. Sounds like a plan. I can't believe I have

to tell another family we lost the body."

James squeezed her shoulder. "We'll figure it out. I promise."

She tried to smile but it wouldn't come. "I'm going to check upstairs to see if there's anything misplaced."

"All right. I'll get things rolling down here. This isn't going to happen again. I promise."

"Hope not," she replied, climbing the stairs with purpose. She wanted to get in Rick's room before he came back from running errands—if that's really what he was up to.

When she approached Shanna's bedroom, she looked behind her to make sure James hadn't followed her. He probably wouldn't appreciate her fishing around in his buddy's stuff.

The coast is clear.

Lily breathed in as she stood at the door.

There's a smell.

Not a rotten one but a sharp burnt odor mixed with a hint of the floral room spray her sister always used. As she opened the door, her shoulders relaxed. Nothing looked odd or out of place—not that she believed the missing bodies would be in this room, but she felt slightly better about barging in and finding nothing.

Lily quickly rifled through the drawers in Shanna's cabinet. She found nothing but his folded clothing. As she went through his stuff, she noticed he'd brought very little with him. Although Rick hadn't been completely transparent about how long he would be staying, it didn't seem like it would be for a long time.

She checked the bathroom. Nothing was out of the ordinary there. Then she stood in the center of the room, scanning every corner until her eyes landed on a black bag next to the bed on the opposite side of the door. She rushed over to take a look at it. Rick could be headed up the stairs for all she knew.

She needed to search the bag.

As soon as her hands pulled out what looked to be a black shirt, the same odd smell smacked her in the face. Her nasal passages stung. She suppressed the urge to cough. This is where the burnt smell was coming from—as if Rick had been around a bonfire recently. But she detected something else in the odor, something she dealt with all the time at work, something familiar.

The rancid charred stench was unmistakable. She smelled a burnt body. Knowing she would need the shirt for evidence at a later time, she rushed to hide it in Shanna's closet under some extra linen. Then she scrambled out of the bedroom and made her way to her office before anyone could see her. As she processed what she'd found, Lily sank into the cushioning support of her leather chair. She'd never felt more positive about any other case.

Detective Rick Drakon, friend of James, was Zeus.

Chapter Six

James stared down at the forensics report on his desk. Ms. Bernardo was the second body snatched. They searched the entire premises and found no trace of her. The questions remained, who would steal a body? And how were they being transported out from under everyone's nose? He'd seen some sick stuff in his time in The City, but this had strange written all over it.

He couldn't help but wonder if someone out there was targeting Lily again. Owning a successful business had no doubt brought out the crazies and made her have to watch her back. But with nothing to go on he couldn't even formulate a theory.

A knock on his door shook him out of his thoughts. "Come in."

Don Abrams came in, a big smirk on his face. "I couldn't resist the need for an update on Mr. or Ms. Body Snatcher. Did you catch him or her yet?" He plopped down in the seat across from James.

"Not with this kind of forensics. No fingerprints, hair fibers or blood found at the scene."

"Those are my favorite type."

"It gets better. I can't find Sam, the ritual recruiter."

Abrams frowned. "Who?"

"The guy who approached Demetri Popov to join a cult with human sacrifice. Except instead of a live sacrifice they're using the bodies taken from Reynolds Funeral Home."

Abrams shook his head. "Come again?"

"See, I knew you'd agree it's crazy."

"Well, I've seen some things but stealing bodies from a funeral home is of the lowest quality. Who is Demetri Popov?"

"A lead I've been trying to suss out. He's the one who led me down this rabbit hole. I bet the recruiter, Sam, isn't his real name anyway. It seems like he's the phantom recruiter I'll never find. The other day I stood outside Saint Nicholas Church for hours hoping someone would try to recruit me into the cult."

Abrams smiled. "You don't exactly have innocent victim written all over you. You should send someone with less tattoos and hair gel."

"Ha! Like whom?" James pointed at Abrams. "You? You're right. You do have docile grandpa vibes. When are you available to come with me?"

Abrams chuckled. "You're hysterical. I'm too old for stakeouts. Anyway, if you do find him you think he'll talk?"

"Probably not."

"What else you got?"

"Apparently, Zachary was the last one to see the body after moving it from the embalming room to the make-up room."

"That's not insignificant. Did you talk to him?" Abrams asked.

"Of course. He didn't break a sweat. He transported her and went back to his other tasks."

"Can anyone corroborate that information?"

"No, no one else was around except Lily."

"If you ask me, he's not completely off the list."

James scowled. "Again we're pointing fingers at the Reynolds family? What would his motivation be?"

"Money. Maybe someone is paying him to take the bodies. He doesn't care what happens to them. They're already dead."

James shook his head. "That doesn't sit right. Not too long ago, Zachary was almost murdered. That does something to a person."

"Yeah, it makes them angry."

"It might but that doesn't equate to turning into a criminal. Plus, we've been down this road before. It's still the wrong road."

"I think it demonstrates how suspiciously he behaves—"

"Or," James said with a tap of his pen on the table, "you're in a continuous loop that never goes anywhere because it takes more effort to look elsewhere."

No response. Abrams's expression went stone cold.

Too far?

They'd had an altercation in the past, but Abrams had been drunk, very drunk. It hardly counted.

Abrams's eyes avoided looking directly at James. "Look, I call it like I see it. That's how I was trained. Even though you are under my wing—"

"*Was,* I was under your wing."

"You seem to march to your own drum. So, it doesn't matter what I say anyway."

"I get it. I get it. It's the most obvious path and usually the right one but . . . not this time." James blew out the air in his lungs.

"And everyone else was accounted for?"

"Supposedly. Lily, of course, is protective of her

team but I wonder about Chris Tuchman. Does anyone really know anything about him? He did work closely with Tina Collins who almost took down the whole business last year. And how are they getting the bodies out? It points to an inside job."

"True. If you're worried about Chris, you should look into it."

"He and Marcia Alonso are the wild cards of the group."

"But you don't think Marcia is capable of such a thing?"

"I wouldn't start with her. I've done a little snooping into Chris already. He's single, and lives with a roommate in a house off of Stuart Road. He has no record. He grew up a little farther north and graduated at the head of his class."

"He does seem young to manage a business."

"That's not illegal."

"No, it's not." Abrams leaned in. "So what you're saying is you have nothing on him?"

"Yet. I don't have anything on him yet but I do plan on talking with the roommate, Stan. He seemed eager to talk."

"There's probably a feud there that has nothing to do with the case."

"Maybe, but I chase all leads."

"You know what they say? All leads lead to heaven." Abrams pointed his thumb up in the air.

"Or hell. Have I mentioned I hate this case?"

"That's because it hits too close to home. Speaking of home, how's married life?"

James paused to reflect. All in all things were pretty good. He knew he had to manage his own fears and let

Lily be herself even if that meant biting his tongue when she wanted to jump right in front of a train. "Married life is good. You should try it sometime."

Abrams smiled wide. "Is that right? Don't judge so hard. You never know what's around the corner."

James's right eyebrow shot up. "I'll take that as a maybe."

"Have you gone on your honeymoon yet? Seems like a break from the funeral home might do you two some good."

"Leaving the investigation unsolved to go on a trip isn't ideal but I have been working on something."

Abrams's eyebrows shot up. "What's that?"

James returned a coy smile. "It's a surprise."

****

Lily stared out at the patrol car stationed on the opposite street from her bedroom window. She could barely see the driver's face in the fading light. It didn't matter. The person of interest may be spending the night in their house. And she fully intended on pursuing the strange ritual theory with Rick as the ringleader. Naturally, her suspicions would not go over well with James. In fact, she had not quite figured out how to tell him. But her instincts hadn't and wouldn't lead her astray. At least she hoped.

"How was your day?"

She looked over her shoulder at James as he entered the room. "Not the best. I had to tell Ms. Bernardo's family the bad news. I told them we were working as hard as possible to get the body back but I'm not so optimistic."

We aren't getting the body back. It was burned.

"I haven't found much either, but someone had to

have seen something. The thief simply strolled into the funeral home—I'm guessing through the garage—and carried a body out from under everyone's nose? This person is not acting alone or . . . it's an inside job."

Her stare could slice through his heart. "It's very possible he is not acting alone."

"Zachary was the last person to see the body."

"Zachary?" Her hands went to her hips. "Who suggested him? You?"

"No, I defended him. I had a conversation with Abrams about this case and Zachary's name came up."

"As what? A suspect?"

"Not really. We were talking about who had been around the body at the time it was taken. His name came up. We were being thorough."

"I'm sure Abrams told you to look into it. Seems like something he would do."

"It's not personal. You should know that by now. I don't think Zachary's involved but we have to look at every angle."

"Every angle? What about Rick? He's an *angle* you haven't looked into yet."

"He wasn't even here when it went down." James gestured toward her. "That's what you told me. I know you're unhappy with his unexpected visit but let's not blame a perfectly straight up detective for the crime."

Lily sucked in a breath. She knew her outing Rick wouldn't get her anywhere today, but she wanted to plant the seed before trying her theory in the field. "I talked to Chris today."

"What about?" James asked as he took his shoulder holster off and hung it on the chair in front of the vanity.

"I thought since he's the manager he'd have insight

on how Marcia and the others were doing."

"And?" He took his time emptying his pockets onto his nightstand. Keys, lip ointment and assorted coins clanged on the table's surface.

"He said he had no concerns about them. Marcia's work has been on point and Antonio seemed happy with the client load. Neither felt overworked or underappreciated." She shrugged her shoulders. "I suspected as much since I pride myself in providing a comfortable workplace for everyone."

"I have no doubts about that either. But what about him? Have *you* any concerns about Chris?"

She stared out into the diminishing light outside her window. "I guess I should have some concerns given where he came from, but my gut says he's not involved."

"Your *gut* is usually right but there's nothing wrong—"

"With being thorough. I know. I know." She remained facing the window.

"Listen, I know this has been frustrating." He reached his arms out and rubbed her upper back and neck. "You need a break, a warm, sunny break."

The muscles in her neck loosened as he massaged them. Her mind drifted from the funeral home to a deserted island where her skin would sizzle deliciously under the hot sun. "That would be nice."

"Good. Pack your bags."

Her eyes snapped open. "What?"

"We're going to Hawaii."

She turned to him. "What are you talking about?"

"Our honeymoon. We haven't gone yet. I figured now is a good time to get away."

"How is now a good time to get away? Two bodies

have gone missing. We're in the middle of an investigation."

"I think we can give Rick the low down and let him take over for a few days. He's a detective just like…us."

She crossed her arms. "You mean he's a detective like you, not me."

"No, you're just as capable but you're not quite on the payroll—"

"And what about that? I thought you were going to handle that issue."

He grabbed her hands gently, bringing her attention to his face. "I will. I promise."

How could she stay mad? Her entire being had always fallen into his eyes whenever she looked at them. Today was no exception. She forced her shoulders to relax. Leaving Rick behind in her funeral home did not bring her any comfort.

"I love that you want to go on a honeymoon and that you planned something special for us. I'm simply not sure now is a good time."

"It's the perfect time. Rick is here. He'll take over the case while we're gone and look after the funeral home. It's a perfect setup."

Her heart sank. If only it had been someone other than Rick, his plan would've been perfect. "So this was the plan all along with Rick staying with us?"

He put her hands on his chest and wiggled his hips. "I've been scheming up a storm."

She smiled at his enthusiasm, but the dark matter of Rick weighed heavily on her mind. How could she leave that man alone with her family and her business while she went to paradise? It would not work.

She would have to solve the case before the trip, or

it would be impossible for her to fathom leaving everything in the hands of Rick Drakon.

"When do we leave?"

"Seven days."

Chapter Seven

Lily's original plan had been to watch Rick like a hawk and hope he did something incriminating in front of her, but instead she found herself staring at Zachary. She watched him grimace as he lifted boxes of inventory to stock up the embalming room with supplies. It'd been almost a year since he'd been brutally stabbed right outside the funeral home's front door. His recovery had been fairly quick, but she wondered if he'd rushed back to work a little prematurely. Before she could offer some help, she noticed Rick had beat her to it.

"Hey, let me help you with those," Rick announced as he entered the embalming room.

She wanted to hear more, so she figured organizing the hall linen closet right then and there seemed like a good idea. As she pulled out a couple of towels to fold a bit neater, she overheard their conversation.

"How's it going?" Rick asked Zachary.

"Not bad." He responded. "Trying to get some of this grunt work out of the way."

"Isn't everything you do grunt work?"

She heard Zachary laugh. "I'm glad you're here, man. Things are less boring."

"Oh, so I'm purely here for your entertainment," Rick replied.

"Something like that."

She also heard Rick's laugh. Her heart sank. The

man seemed to be filling the role of father figure for her brother. That's all she needed, a detective with a gruesome ancient ritual side hustle, taking Zachary under his wing. It was happening right under her roof, and she needed to stop it.

"I'm glad I'm serving some purpose while I'm here," Rick said. "We should play hoops later. You need to redeem yourself from last time."

"You cheated."

"That's what they all say. But that's fine. You need a little practice that's all."

"Is that right?"

"I'd be happy to offer you some pointers and share my expertise."

"Wow, listen to you. Where'd you get all that confidence?"

"I was born with it."

"Must be nice. Blind confidence."

"Hey, stick with me and soon you'll be making all the right moves."

Lily snorted—all the right moves to jail. She shook her head in disappointment. Had she neglected Zachary? Was he really this easy to manipulate?

"Sounds good I guess," Zachary replied.

"Are you sure you don't need any help?"

"Yeah, I'm almost done with this. Next, I'm going to break down the cardboard boxes."

"Seems like you need a promotion," Rick said.

Lily seethed. Who the heck was he? Putting things in Zachary's mind to win him over and go against her. Rick, for sure, needed to go.

"Yeah," Zachary chuckled. "Maybe you can put in a good word for me."

"I will. Listen, I'll hit you up later for grub."

"All right, later."

Lily continued to straighten the linens in the closet as Rick walked past her. He hadn't noticed her deep in the closet as he headed upstairs. She waited until she heard him shut Shanna's door before she entered the embalming room.

"How's it going, Zach? Need help?" Lily kneeled down to grab bottles of embalming fluid out of the box.

"Nah, I'm good."

"How are things with your girlfriend?"

"Julie's good. She's always worried about me though."

"Is she worried about your safety working here?"

Zachary glanced at Lily. The family business was a touchy subject. "After what happened last year, I don't blame her. But now you've got even more security on hand to keep people in check."

"More security?"

"Yeah. Isn't that why Rick's here? To help us out?"

"Sort of. James thought Rick could watch over the business while he and I went on our honeymoon. I'm not sure he really thought it through though."

"Honeymoon? Where are you guys going?"

"Hawaii."

"Wow. Can I come?"

"No, sorry. I'm not even sure if we should go."

"Why not? It seems like James has it all figured out and you'll have a good time getting away from everything here."

"We would have a good time but how can I trust Rick with our business? I don't know him from some random guy off the street."

"He's not a random person off the street. He's a friend and a detective. Is there a better combo?"

Lily changed her tone. "You like him, huh?"

"What's not to like? He plays hoops with me. The other day he showed me how to barbecue ribs on the grill with his secret sauce. And he listens to me. I'm not sure what your beef is with him but so far he's been a pretty upstanding guy."

Lily rubbed her temples. Hearing all this devotion to Rick brought on a headache. "You know you can always do that stuff with James. He's always available."

"James is not always available. I've never once seen him show any interest in sports or grilling."

"All right, but I'm sure there are things that you two would both be interested in if you took the time to figure it out."

"James doesn't have time. He's always on call. The last time we went out to dinner he had to leave before he finished his entree."

Lily bit the insides of her cheeks. He wasn't wrong. She couldn't argue with him, but she needed to push him in the opposite direction—away from evil. "True, but I think both of you can try harder. I'll talk to James about it. But I get it. I don't know Rick like you do."

"Well, you should try harder to get to know him. Not everyone out there is trying to destroy the family business."

A lump formed in her throat. That stung. But that was exactly how she felt, under attack. She tapped his shoulder. "Don't you worry. Before we leave for our honeymoon, I'll make an effort to get to know him and make sure we are all on the same page."

She left her brother to his work, but she already

knew more than enough about Rick. It broke her heart that Zachary had bonded with a criminal. Her job, along with Shanna, was to protect the family and the business and she would do it at whatever the cost, even if it made her the bad guy.

Chapter Eight

"Tonight? I'd love to. What time?"

As she approached the make-up room, Lily heard Marcia having a one-sided conversation. She wanted to update her on their newest client—the fact that they still had a business despite the missing bodies was nothing short of a miracle—but instead of knocking, as she should've done, she stopped in front of the door to eavesdrop. Due to Marcia's timid nature, Lily felt as if she knew so little about her, even a little hint into her life would be helpful—at least that's what she told herself.

"You're new in town," Marcia said. "How about if I pick the place?"

Lily's ears perked. This sounded like a date. She wondered who the guy was and if she knew him. Given the size of Manorview there weren't many options.

"Marco's has great Italian food but don't expect too much. I know you're used to eating well in New York City. I can make an eight o'clock reservation. Does that sound good?"

Lily's imagination exploded. The guy was new to town and from New York City. So was Rick Drakon. Marcia and Rick are going on a date? Lily's stomach burned as she retreated to her office to properly compose herself. She sat at her desk and hid her face in her palms.

Rick and Marcia?

When did all that happen? And what would he want

from Marcia? It made perfect sense to her that Rick would pick the weakest sheep in the flock to spill company secrets—not to mention the father-figure relationship he'd started with Zachary. Clearly, Rick knew what he was doing—infiltrating her family and business like a disease for easier access to the bodies. Lily rubbed her eyes and sucked in a breath.

Now, she had to do something about it.

****

Hours later, Lily swept the final layer of peach blush over her raised cheek bones under James's watchful eye in the background of her vanity mirror.

"Gina is having a launch party at her store?" he asked in a calm manner.

Lies. Lies.

"Uh-huh. She's launching her own hair color line." Lily answered without looking at him—not completely untrue. Gina Giordani, owner of Beauty Bazaar where Lily purchased all the makeup products she needed for her business and good friend, had always said she wanted to do something like that. Someday.

"I shouldn't be too long, but I wanted to show my support. It's not every day that someone starts a new business."

Lily rose to give James a kiss before she left. The faster she got out of the house, the better. She reached up to put her arms around him. He barely returned her affection. She sensed his reluctance but was too deep into the ploy to jump off the boat now.

"Be careful. We've got a body snatcher out there."

"Luckily, they only snatch the dead ones."

His eyes were cold and lifeless. "You never know. Maybe they'll move on to the living."

Lily smiled. "There you go again, worrying. And all I'm doing is going to a party."

He doesn't believe me.

Her stomach turned inside out.

White lies. They're just a couple of white lies.

He would forgive her once she uncovered Rick's true identity. As an ace detective, she knew he would overlook this one tiny moment to nail a bad guy—even if the bad guy was his friend.

Lily grabbed her faux croc evening bag and turned one last time toward her husband, hoping against all odds that he'd gotten over his fears. "I'll be home soon."

He looked at her stone-faced. "Call if you need me."

"Sounds good but I won't need you." She smiled and walked toward the stairs, taking them two at a time.

"I hope not."

From the doorway she heard him moving about the upper floor as she grabbed her car keys. It was just a couple of hours undercover. What could possibly go wrong?

It took only minutes for Lily to get to Marco's. She parked her car on one of the side streets. Her plan to infiltrate Marcia's date with Rick and make it look like a coincidence, was not the best one ever contrived.

Marco's offered good Italian food. She'd been there countless times so she knew as she walked in that the bar would be on the left and the dining tables flared out to the right facing the front windows. As she entered under the dim lighting, she scanned the bustling room for her target and scored a hit immediately.

Far off in the right-hand corner, Marcia sat, facing the front door. Her brawny bald companion sat across from her. Before her eyes could connect with Marcia's,

Lily turned to the bar to order a drink. She squeezed herself in between a group of women chatting away, and a couple deep in conversation with each other.

"Good evening, Lily. Nice to see you tonight. What can I get you?" Chad, the bartender asked as he placed a small napkin in front of her.

"Hey, Chad. Thought I'd come in for a quick sip."

"What'll it be? The usual?"

"Definitely."

Liquid courage.

When Chad came back with a dry martini, she took a big gulp. She might be taking a risk, but it didn't have to be all terrible. The vodka burned her throat. She chased it with an olive. The sharp vinegar paired well. After one last sip, she got up and walked over to the couple. Her heart thundered in her ears. She had no idea how this would go but her instinct told her Rick had to be stopped.

Dodging waiters as they either took orders or served steaming plates of food, Lily approached their table. Marcia looked up; shock replaced her usual timid demeanor.

"Good evening, folks," Lily said, putting false cheer into her voice. "When I stopped in for a drink, I didn't expect to see you two together."

Lily grabbed a chair from a table that had just been vacated and pulled herself into their table. She set her martini glass down in front of her and watched their faces process her presence. She expected Marcia's look of terror but the fleeting glimpse of anger on Rick's face took her by surprise. He'd always maintained a happy outlook but now she'd clearly irked him.

"We're having a bite to eat," he said, pushing his

empty plate toward the middle of the table. "What brings you here, all alone?"

"I come in here sometimes for a drink after work. I've known Chad, the bartender, for years. He makes a good martini but then I looked over and spotted you two and thought I'd say hey." This time, Lily looked at Marcia for clues. Her cheeks looked flushed, and she avoided eye contact. "Is this a date?"

"We're all working so closely in one house, I'd thought it'd be nice to get out," Rick said. "No harm in that."

"Certainly, no harm at all," Lily said. "The tiramisu is fabulous."

Now they know that she knows. Lily hoped that would be enough to stop Rick from pursuing Marcia any further or maybe Marcia would now be worried enough about losing her job that she'd decide to stay away from Rick.

"I think we're all set here." Rick stated. "It's getting late, and I should drive Marcia home to get some sleep before her long workday tomorrow." He gestured toward Lily's martini. "You have quite a bit left to drink. I hope you don't mind if we take off?"

"Not at all. James will be by shortly and Chad usually keeps me company."

"Great. See you back at home," Rick said, also avoiding eye contact.

The two scurried out of the restaurant. He let Marcia lead the way while he followed behind in a protective manner. They could pretend all they want, Lily decided, but something was going on between them.

After they left, Lily took her drink with her to the bar where Chad wiped down the counter and produced yet another small napkin for her drink. His spikey blonde hair gave him a youthful look, but she knew better, he'd been working at Marco's forever.

He smiled at her. "Your friends left mighty quickly."

She took a long sip. It was time to go home. "I guess they don't like me that much."

"Guess not. It's like my wife always says, keep your friends close and your enemies closer."

"And boy are they close."

Chad smiled again and moved over to the couple that had just sat down at the bar. She wanted to give Rick and Marcia time to get home and avoid the awkwardness. As the boss in the house, she knew Marcia would be struggling with embarrassment.

Ten more minutes went by before Lily finally got up and waved to Chad. "Thanks for the company and superb drink. Until next time."

Chad saluted. "Aye, aye. Until then."

Lily left the restaurant and walked toward her car. The cool fall breeze circled her neck and went down her back. With winter approaching, a honeymoon in Hawaii seemed like the perfect getaway. She wanted to feel excited about the trip, but she had to solve the case first, or at the very least get Rick out of her life.

As she approached her vehicle where it was parked under a streetlight, she sensed something was off. Her car was lower to the ground. She came around to the side to get a better look. That's when she noticed the right back tire was completely flat.

Ugh. "I have a flat tire? When did that happen?" Then she noticed the tire on the front was also flat.

All of them?

Whipping around to the other side of her car she saw the rest were flat, too.

"No way," she said to no one.

While the quiet of the side street enveloped her, she searched the surrounding area. Marco's wasn't on the main drag of the town, therefore patrons had to park on the side streets. Goosebumps dotted her arms. She didn't hear anything out of the ordinary even though the tire slasher might still be nearby, waiting to kidnap her. Thankfully, she heard no footsteps or rustling anywhere.

Calm down, Lily.

She pulled out her phone to call for help. Of course her first instinct was to call James, but he'd be pissed she'd gotten herself into trouble again and she'd have to admit she'd lied to him about where she'd gone tonight. She had no doubt Rick had something to do with her flat tires but surely James wouldn't agree. With no other good options, she dialed his number anyway while a massive lump formed in her throat.

He'll forgive me, right?

Chapter Nine

James leaned out of his car window, staring up at Lily. "Launch party, huh?"

She bit her lip and hung her head in shame. He hadn't believed her story in the first place. If he knew Lily, she'd been out tonight chasing some theory and wound up in trouble. He wondered how much trouble he could handle. "Get in. Any idea who would slash your tires?"

Lily walked around to the passenger side and entered the vehicle. She hadn't looked him in the eyes yet. "Yes, I have a theory but you're not going to like it." Her eyelashes fluttered as she glanced at him.

The silver-grey of her eyes lit up the darkness around them. He struggled to stay mad at her for lying and getting herself into trouble. "I know I'm not going to like it. That's the basis of our entire relationship. And I'll still try and stop you."

"Well, you're *really* not going to like it this time."

James couldn't even bring himself to drive. Even though cars would have to go around them, he put the car back in park and leaned back in the seat, waiting for the news that might change their relationship forever. His heart began to thud in anticipation.

"Marcia and Rick are dating."

James smiled, and then let out a chuckle. "That dirty

dog. I knew he'd find someone eventually but not right under our own roof." He chuckled a bit more but then stopped when Lily's expression remained unamused.

"Exactly," she said coldly. "Don't you think it's odd he chose someone working for us?"

"No, what I think is odd is picking you up here because someone you've clearly bothered has slashed your tires."

"James, it's Rick. He slashed my tires. You're right, I did not go to Gina's hair care launch party and I'm sorry I lied to you. But I had a good reason."

His right eyebrow rose. "What are you talking about?"

"Earlier today I overheard Marcia talking to him on the phone about going to dinner tonight and I thought I could catch them red-handed."

"You could catch them doing what? Going out to eat? You're telling me that my good friend, Rick—who is currently staying with us so that he can babysit your business while we go on our honeymoon—slashed your tires because you found him eating with Marcia?"

Lily swallowed. "Yes, that's what I'm telling you. I think Rick is not who you think. And I believe he's using Marcia and us to further his cause."

"*His cause*?" James's head pounded. He hoped she wasn't about to tell him what he feared she might say. "Let me get this straight. You think he's the body snatcher?"

"I think it's very possible that he is the body snatcher." She said it without looking at him.

"Lily, I will help with this case, but I will not consider Rick as a suspect. I think you've gone too far this time. We all feel the pressure to solve the case, but this is way beyond credible."

Her arms went out. "Then who would slash my tires?"

"We can try to collect any surveillance video from homes or businesses in the vicinity of your car; we'll also check to see if anything was left behind. Who knows? Maybe you really pissed off the wrong person."

She nodded. "I did. It was Rick."

"Did he run out of the restaurant in between courses to come and slash your tires and then run back to have dessert?"

"Kind of. They did leave rather abruptly. I don't think they even had dessert."

"So then he ran over to your car with Marcia—a trustworthy employee—slashed your tires as she looked on and got out of there before you were the wiser."

"Yes, that's exactly what happened. Who among us really knows Marcia that well?"

"I'm fine with you checking her out. But your theory that Rick is some cult leader, stealing bodies out of a funeral home is way off."

James put the car in gear and drove toward the next light. His heart sank as he felt the wedge growing between them. He knew she would pursue this until the end—whatever that meant—but he didn't know how it would impact their relationship.

"James, I promise I won't lie to you again, but I am going to follow my instincts."

"I know you will." He paused. "Now Rick knows you suspect him. How's that going to work? He's supposed to be babysitting the funeral home while we go on our honeymoon. Why would he even bother now?"

"He doesn't know I think he's the body snatcher. All

I did was call them out for dating, which as her boss, is not that strange. Plus, Shanna can babysit the funeral home."

"I wanted to leave some muscle behind while we were away and you're not going to win any popularity contests for outing people."

"It's a good thing I was never popular and therefore, I don't care about that."

"*You* weren't popular in school?"

From the corner of his eye he noticed her staring his way. "Me? The red-headed girl whose parents were murdered in their sleep? Oh, yeah, I was the belle of the ball back in the day."

He said nothing. He wanted to tell her that in his eyes, she won all the popularity contests that ever existed. She held the number one spot in his heart. But he couldn't. She lied to him and almost sabotaged his honeymoon plans for a crazy theory involving his friend. He couldn't pretend to be supportive. "I hope you'll consider the consequences of your actions, Lily."

She looked away from him. "It will all make sense in the end."

"I hope you're right."

****

He was mad. She hated that, but in her heart, she knew she was right. Once James realized it, he would forgive her for everything. And he didn't need to know about her dirty tactics either.

Or so she hoped as she stared at Marcia's purse in the funeral home's kitchen, trying to resist the urge to rifle through it. The back of her neck prickled with anxiety. As Marcia's employer, Lily knew what she was about to do was wrong but at this point she'd already pissed off enough people, including her husband. Why stop now? Plus, after hiring Marcia when her previous employer went to prison for murder, she felt certain that Marcia needed the Reynolds Funeral Home more than it needed her. Lily would have to see this through the end.

She eyed the simple black canvas tote bag with handles that stuck up in the air. Lily listened for footsteps, but lunch wasn't for a few hours and everyone had already come in and grabbed their morning coffee. Now was a good time for inappropriate behavior.

Unzipping the top portion, she began investigating its contents. A slim navy-blue wallet took up a large amount of space amongst crumpled up paper receipts and face powder. In the smaller compartment she found keys, gum and a pen. Her shoulders slumped. What did she think she would find in there? A treasure map pointing to Rick? A tape-recorded conversation between them revealing who he really was?

She felt foolish—until her fingers landed on a piece of folded paper. Pulling it out, she opened the unassuming document. Her heart thumped once she realized what it was. In her hands Lily held a copy of the Zeus pamphlet James had shown her.

Lily scrambled to analyze it before anyone decided to step in for a snack. The front fold looked exactly the same as the one James had shown her with the lone word *Zeus*. But the inside page had more. Under the picture of the house was one word: *Rubin*.

She knew it! She'd known the abandoned Rubin mansion would be a perfect spot for secluded illegal activities. Now she had proof.

The sound of a door opening down the hall drove her into action. She folded the brochure and stuffed it back in the purse, pulling the zipper closed as fast as possible. Then she opened the fridge and began rifling through the plastic containers for her potato salad.

"Hungry already? It's barely eleven o'clock," Marcia said, tossing a peach pit into the trash and an empty plastic water bottle in the recycle bin.

Lily closed the refrigerator door.

Marcia had a smile on her face. She, apparently, was going to pretend that nothing was bothering her after Lily caught her having dinner with Rick.

"How's the day going for you?" Lily asked.

"Not bad. It's been busy since the shutdown of Innovations Funeral Home. I already did six makeovers and it's not even noon."

"That's pretty good. At least news surrounding the body snatcher hadn't circulated yet."

Marcia returned a generic smile but said nothing.

"And hopefully, there aren't too many things distracting you from your work."

Marcia cocked her head. "No distractions here."

"Well, it wasn't my idea to have Rick stay with us. I hope he's not pestering you. If he is, I can ask him to leave."

Marcia smiled. "He's not bothering me. Quite the contrary."

Lily didn't know this version of Marcia. Last time she checked, the woman acted scared of her own shadow. Dating Rick had given her some gumption, or maybe being part of his cult of weirdoes gave her a boost of confidence? Either way, she had to get to the bottom of things.

She put a hand on Marcia's arm. "I want you to know that I'm here for you. If you feel like you've gotten yourself involved in something that you can't get out of, I can help."

A flicker of recognition shown in Marcia's eyes, then her smile vanished. "Rick has been nothing but good to me." She put her hand flat against her chest. "He saved me from a meaningless existence, and you helped when you gave me this job. I'm so grateful. It was the first step in leaving my past behind. I never knew my father and my mother drank herself to death when I was twelve. You could say I've been alone and lost ever since bouncing around from family member to family member. But after Innovations Funeral Home shut down, you gave me a chance here and that led me to Rick."

Great.

Dread filled Lily's body. The poor girl had gone from the evil incarnate: Tina Collins of Innovations Funeral Home to Rick Drakon, cult leader.

And indirectly, Lily was responsible for it. "I'm sorry you've had such a rough time. I can certainly understand life without a solid family foundation but not everyone is who they seem."

"I am certain Rick has saved me. In fact, I want to spend my whole life with him."

Ugh. Brainwashed.

The only way to get her out of Rick's cult was to get rid of its leader.

"Why do you think he has saved you? You have a good job, a place to live. What is he doing for you that you can't do for yourself?"

"He makes me feel wanted and worth something."

As much as she could try, Lily knew she couldn't argue with her. She knew how it felt to be lost and searching for meaning but she'd been lucky to have

Shanna to keep her in check and the business to keep her busy.

"You can't rely on a man to make you feel worth something. You're worth something without him. In fact, you're probably better off without him."

Marcia smiled respectfully. But the glassy look in her eyes meant she wasn't listening. This felt even more personal. Not only was Rick stealing from her business, but he was also stealing Marcia's soul.

"I appreciate the concern but I'm all right. In fact, I'm great. Rick has been nothing but helpful to everyone and the business as far as I can tell. No need to worry." Marcia shrugged, her entire demeanor nonchalant.

But Lily had no idea what else she could say to save Marcia from Rick. A nervous smile was all she could manage.

"I've got a client waiting for makeup so I better get back to work." With a wave, Marcia left the kitchen.

Lily's heart stung. Marcia sounded so lost. Given the challenges in Marcia's background, she could empathize. Plus, it made it all the harder to investigate her. But if Marcia was just an innocent bystander, Rick wouldn't be bothering with her. He was using her. Lily needed to find out how deeply Marcia was involved.

To do that, she needed to check out the Rubin house.

Chapter Ten

As James pumped the barbell into the air for the twentieth rep, he stared at the massive ceiling fan spinning cool air throughout the workout room. He often went to the gym in the evening to clear his head because there were fewer people around. Tonight he had more than one reason to get his frustrations out. As he'd previously discussed with Abrams, James had decided to look into the Reynolds Funeral Home manager, Chris Tuchman, as a possible suspect for the body snatcher. However his theory had not panned out.

Largely going on a hunch, he had spoken to Stan, the roommate, and found nothing useful to pursue. Stan complained about Chris like a jealous schoolgirl but hadn't produced a single piece of useful or incriminating information. As much as James wanted to point the finger at Chris it was hard to admit that maybe he'd pushed for an easy victory. Who could blame him? His wife was convinced his buddy had done it—no wonder he was grasping at straws.

His muscles ached as he pushed air out of his lungs under the weight of the bar, rep after rep. After hooking the bar back on the rack, he sat up. Sweat dribbled from his neck down his chest, plastering his once white T-shirt to his skin. As he looked up to grab the towel hanging on the bench press rack, he caught his wife watching him.

"See anything you like?"

A wicked grin appeared on her face. "Always."

She sat on the bench press next to his—her skin looked as radiant as ever, even in the harsh gym lighting. Despite how she made him feel, he couldn't shake his annoyance that she'd lied to him.

"How's your day been?" she asked.

He lay back on the bench. "Not bad." Grabbing the bar and pulling it off the rack he pumped and grunted through five reps before resting the bar back on the hook. Out of breath and fatigued he wiped his forehead with the towel.

Her eyes glowed with intensity. "I found out something interesting today—a really good lead."

He loved it when she had that look—it meant she was happy. This time, he hoped she hadn't gone too far. "Did you do anything illegal to get this lead?"

"No, since no one caught me."

He tried to restrain himself, but the smile forced itself onto his face. He quickly shut it down. "Are you expecting me to bail you out this time?"

A loud thud from a barbell hitting the floor across the room made her jump. Her silver-gray eyes looked briefly at the ceiling, as she seemed to contemplate her answer. "The possibility of that cannot be ruled out. But it will be worth it." She held her hands out. "Can I tell you why?"

He watched her enthusiastic display and could barely stay mad.

Play it cool.

Clearing his throat he ran his hands through his hair—the strands in the front refused to stay back. "Fine. Tell me."

She cocked her head. "Still mad?" She got up and

sat on his bench—inches away.

He was mad at her, but he was still a man. No matter what was going on in their relationship, his body responded when she came near him. And that dang lavender shampoo made him almost forget he was upset. He breathed it in anyway, succumbing to her power over him.

"How can I make it better?" she teased near his ear. Her hand rubbed his aching shoulder.

"That's a good start."

"I'm sorry. I won't lie to you again," she murmured. Then she moved her hand down his back in long strokes up and down, kneading his tight muscles.

He let out a groan. "You should come to the gym with me more often."

"I can do that after I find my body snatcher."

He sighed, unable to stand his ground any longer. "Tell me."

Her hands continued to work the taut sinew, making him lean into her as far as he could.

"I found something in Marcia's purse."

He straightened his back, stopping her hands. "You went through an employee's purse? I'm pretty sure that's illegal."

"Details. Plus, I had reasonable suspicion she was up to something. The gamble paid off."

"One day your luck will run out and you'll find yourself on the wrong end of a gun paying for your mistake."

"All right, Professor Safety-First. Are you done with the lecture? Can I tell you what I found?"

James already felt more relaxed now that he'd said what he needed to say—the massage also helped. "You don't have to stop," he gestured toward his back.

"You're really something," she said but resumed the massage. "I found evidence that connects her to the body snatcher."

"I'm listening."

"She had a copy of the Zeus flyer in her bag."

"The Zeus flyer? You mean the weird ritual one that Demetri Popov gave me?"

"The same one."

He paused, uncertain of the connection but taken aback. He hadn't expected to hear about that again. "Whoever is passing them out is certainly persistent."

Her hands stopped working his back and she stood up to face him. "Whoever is passing them out is part of a cult that deals in human sacrifices."

"And now you think Marcia is part of the cult?"

"Yes. She got recruited and is now an accomplice to the body snatching. She works at my funeral home. How can she not be a part of it?"

He looked down at his feet. He didn't want to go on. "So she was recruited the same way Demetri was? Near the church?"

Her sigh was unmistakable. "You know very well that's not how she got recruited."

He looked up at her. Fire-red hair framed her silver-dagger eyes. Her arms crossed over her chest and one foot tapped with impatience. An involuntary ache ravaged his stomach. The can of worms he'd been trying so hard to keep sealed would now burst open.

James leaned back on his arms, resigned to whatever came next. "Rick."

She softened her stance. She knew she'd won.

"If you're right, you better hurry up," he warned.

"Our honeymoon is right around the corner. You wouldn't want to leave him alone in that funeral home with so many bodies." The sarcasm oozed.

"Don't worry. I have a plan."

"Are you going to let me in on it?"

"Of course not."

"I figured. So you told me your news. Now what?"

She came closer. Her thighs rubbed up against his knees. He looked up at her. The same ache he always had near her returned. She stared down at him. "Still mad?"

He looked away and smiled, giving in. "No." Then he took her hand and pulled her to him until her lips were on his. The kiss went deeper, satisfying a hungry need. Relief swept through his body. It had been a while.

She lingered another second and then pulled away. "You should be mad at me more often."

"Something tells me that will happen sooner rather than later. Besides, I have some news myself."

Her hands went to her hips. "Oh, really? Are you keeping things from me?"

"You're not the only one with secrets."

Her jaw dropped open.

He wanted to keep the ruse going but her reaction made him chuckle. "Relax, it's not a secret, just some unwelcome investigational news."

"Let's hear it."

James leaned back on the bench. "It seems we were not able to collect any surveillance on the night of your tire attack. You parked in a secluded area. There were no recordings."

Her head fell back. "Ugh. We can't catch a break in this case. Can we?"

"Maybe there's no connection between the tire

slashing and the body snatching." He cracked a smile. "Maybe there wasn't one to begin with."

Lily glared at him. "Maybe you need to do some push-ups. Drop and give me fifty."

James laughed out loud but obeyed her command. He stretched his body out in a plank position and without skipping a beat pumped his arms up and down one after another.

"All right. I'll see you back and the house."

"Ten, eleven, twelve, thirteen," he counted out loud. "Sounds good, Lily. Fourteen, fifteen, sixteen, seventeen."

When he looked up, he found she was gone.

Flipping over on his back he stared at the ceiling as he tried to slow his breathing. He realized he hadn't actually gotten anywhere with Lily. She was still on the same track toward danger, and he'd done nothing to stop it. He breathed out and smacked his fist on the floor. It seemed like he always landed here, acquiescent. But the hard truth was, in order to keep her safe he knew he would need to try harder.

At least, that was the plan.

Chapter Eleven

Shanna stormed into Lily's office. "I'm engaged!"

Lily quickly slid the Zeus pamphlet under her client folders and got up to embrace her sister. "Oh my gosh. I can't believe my ears—to Detective Donald Abrams?"

Shanna frowned. "Who else would it be?"

"No one." Lily shrugged. "But I still can't believe it. Let me see the ring."

Shanna put out her left hand, letting the light catch the sparkle coming from the round stone.

"It's a beauty. Congratulations. I had my doubts that Abrams could be into anything other than himself, but I guess I was wrong."

Shanna playfully wacked Lily on the shoulder. "Oh stop. I knew it all along. All those years of wearing him down finally paid off."

"When did he propose?"

"Last night. I had a feeling something was up when he offered to cook. Best steak I've had in years."

Lily's eyebrows shot up. "Wow. Don Abrams cooked? That *is* serious."

Shanna giggled like a schoolgirl. "I know. It's like he's a different person."

"Have you thought about the wedding date or venue?"

"No. I've barely gotten over the proposal. I know we

don't want anything too flashy but we're not getting any younger so the sooner the better."

Lily's eyes opened wide. "I know! We could do the wedding here. I can plan it for you. You won't have to do anything."

"Here?" Shanna's eyes darted around. "With all the bodies?"

"Why not? You spend almost all your waking hours around them. You used to live and eat here amongst them. If you're comfortable enough to do that, why not get married here?"

Shanna stood in silence. "I guess I always had the traditional venue in mind but now that I think about it, you're right. It would be a lot less expensive, too."

"If you get married next spring, we could do the ceremony outside in the front yard. It's a beautiful house. We should take advantage of it."

Shanna pressed her pointer finger to her lips. "It's not a bad idea. It might take some work convincing Abrams though."

"You're clearly a pro at that and you know what's also a good idea?"

"What?"

"Letting paying customers use the funeral home as their wedding venue as well." Lily's eyes glittered with excitement. "This could be a new source of revenue for us. We already have the vendors for flowers, caterers and music. This is a no-brainer."

Shanna frowned. "It is?"

Lily ignored Shanna's comment as her mind raced with the possibilities. Her eyes went wide. "We could have Chris officiate."

"I thought this was about my wedding?"

"It is, but don't you want to make more money and secure the business for your kids' future?"

"Whoa." Shanna's hands went up. "Kids? Can we just talk about lace or tulle first?"

"All right. I'll reel it in, but I am going to get started on drafting promotional materials, updating our website, etc. We can call it, *Reynolds Royal Weddings*."

"Is it royal though?"

"We're going to make them think it is. I can even do the bride and bridal party's makeup. What would be your contribution? You can't embalm anyone even if the bride wants you to."

"Ha! I can be their point person to help everything get organized."

"But you haven't even had your own wedding yet. You're not qualified."

Shanna cocked her head. "Now you're getting annoying. We'll learn together."

"Fine. I just wanted to make sure you were totally on board."

"I am as long as Zachary doesn't hit on any of the bridesmaids. His breakup with Julie has sent him back to his old ways."

"I know. Poor Zach. They've been dating on and off for a bit now and I think judging by his withdrawn mood lately, they are currently off. We need to keep an eye on him."

Shanna nodded. "What about Marcia? She could help you with the makeup."

Lily's eyes dropped to the ground, avoiding eye contact. "Marcia may be left out of our plans."

"Does this have anything to do with whatever you were hiding from me when I walked in?"

Ah, Shanna. Always on point.

"Maybe. But until I'm sure, I don't want to involve anyone else."

"Does James know?"

"Yes."

"Phew. At least he'll be notified when *your* body turns up."

Lily returned a wicked grin. "We already talked about this. I want to be cremated. I don't want your grubby paws pumping me with formaldehyde."

Shanna pointed at her sister. "You're sick. And keep my groom out of it if you insist on putting yourself in the line of fire."

"I wouldn't dream of involving him. Speaking of which, I think we should go dress shopping as soon as possible, since according to you, I might not be around long enough to help."

"Good idea. I'm ready when you are." Shanna walked to the door but paused in front of it. "What did Marcia do?"

Lily hesitated. She hated all the drama her investigation might cause, knowing it would surely break-up their little group. In the end, it was her fault for hiring Marcia in the first place. She'd been too soft back then. That was about to change.

"Marcia is under investigation."

Chapter Twelve

The lunch crowd on a Thursday at Al's Diner didn't impress James. Months ago he'd noticed the 'D' on the red neon sign outside the place had gone out. And after twenty years in business the scratched plastic booth seats could use a makeover. He often wondered how the place stayed open. It had to be the die-hard loyalists keeping the place alive. Regardless, he was glad to have a place to go for last-minute meetings and at least the food quality was consistent. He'd chosen a corner booth near a window to wait for Rick.

Would he arrive?

He gulped from the glass of ice water in front of him. It didn't surprise him he hadn't seen much of his old friend in the last few days. After Lily accosted Rick with Marcia at the restaurant, James couldn't blame him for laying low. But what exactly was he up to? Did Lily's theory hold any water?

And what should he do about it? Arrest his friend? Call Abrams for backup? Coming out of left field, it all seemed ludicrous. He only hoped Lily was way off the mark.

Ten minutes later, Rick pushed the door open and walked toward his booth. He wore his signature leather jacket and neck chain, but his jeans seemed a bit looser. As he came closer, James saw prominent dark circles under Rick's eyes—a symptom of sleep deprivation? Or something more serious?

"Hey, man," James said as Rick maneuvered into the booth.

"I'm surprised you called." Rick said.

"I'm surprised you came."

Rick smiled.

"How's it going?" James asked as the waiter, came over to take their order. "Hey, Frank, can you bring over some of those loaded nachos with hot sauce on the side?"

"That sounds good," Rick added.

"Not a problem. Anything to drink?" Frank asked, collecting the menus.

"I have a hankering for that peanut butter shake you guys make."

"Another great choice," Rick said. "Make it two."

"Right away." Frank walked away.

"Peanut butter shake? Loaded nachos?" Rick grinned. "Are you feeling all right?"

"Not really but I'm more interested in what you've been up to. I haven't seen you around much."

"I've been meeting up with some friends who have moved upstate over the past year. Plus, Marcia's been keeping me busy." He seemed to be watching for James's reaction.

"You kind of disappeared. I thought I would check in since I'm the one who told you to come up here to do us a favor."

"I'm happy to help. Meeting Marcia was the icing on the cake, but I sense not everyone is pleased by our relationship."

"When you said you wanted to meet someone no one expected it to be Marcia."

Rick put his hand on his chest. "The heart wants

what it wants. And why not her? We met at your place of business. She's an attractive girl." He shrugged his massive shoulders. "What's the big deal?"

James watched his mannerisms. Was this all for show? He'd never known Rick to be a hopeless romantic. He'd always been more interested in his work. What changed?

The hairs on the back of James's neck stood up.

"I bet no one was happy when you started dating your own murder suspect right after you came to town," Rick said.

James's eyebrows shot up. "Crude. But not untrue. The difference is no one suspected me, the detective, of doing anything inappropriate."

"Touché. But I know you agree that small town gossip is a dangerous thing with little credibility."

"I'd agree it's a nuisance, but in this case there really is none. Tell me why Lily might be worried enough about Marcia to track you two down in a restaurant?"

"Marcia comes off as a meek person but there's a lot more to her than people give her credit for. Maybe Lily feels like I'm taking advantage of her but it's not true. She is a perfectly independent woman brimming with artistic and creative talent. I'm happy I met her."

"Marcia aside, is there something about you that has perked up Lily's ears?"

"You know me, James. As soon as someone sees a bald guy with a leather jacket and a gold chain." Rick flicked his necklace. "Automatic trouble."

"I don't think that's what she sees."

Rick opened his hands. "So what does she see?"

"You'll have to ask her yourself. What I do know is you have a past. Growing up around criminals will do things to a person."

"That's like saying no one can overcome his or her past. That means you'll never get over Andrea's death and you'll always be a drug addict."

James's nostrils flared. "That's a low blow and you know it." He struggled to keep his voice down. The last thing he needed to do was pick a fight with Rick at Al's Diner. Plus, Rick was twice his size. A night in the hospital for some unpleasant words seemed unappealing and unnecessary.

"You know I'm right." Rick raised his voice. "I said that to get my point across and I don't like that you've been digging into my background. I have the utmost respect for you but whose side are you on anyway?"

"The side of the law."

"And dating Marcia is certainly not illegal. You know you found nothing on my record."

"I know, but it's also kind of random and Marcia is definitely not your type. You always go for the life of the party. She doesn't fit with what I know about you."

Before Rick could respond, Frank came back with a tray of food. He set down the shakes first and then the large plate of nachos. "Loaded nachos. Just what the doctor ordered. Enjoy."

"Thanks, Frank. Looks good." James said, as he went for his shake.

Rick stared down at the heaping pile of tortilla chips with salsa, refried beans, guacamole and sour cream. "Listen, people change, and paranoia has gotten the best of you. Maybe I want someone to settle down with? Did you ever consider that?" His jaw clenched. "If punching you right now wouldn't hurt my case even more, I wouldn't hesitate for a minute."

"I bet. Look man, you come into town. You find the girl you're least likely to end up with and then you disappear. It's just weird." James popped a chip with fixings dripping off of it into his mouth. The crunch sound filled his ears.

"Well, if being weird is a crime, lock me up. Maybe I'm in love and she's taking up all my time. Don't be jealous." Rick picked off a few chips in rapid-fire bites.

James smiled. "I'm not jealous. But remember, you're here because I invited you."

"All right, I get it. You need more attention. Let me see what I can do to pencil you into my busy schedule." Rick took a long sip of his shake. "Man, that's good."

James felt a headache coming on. He was torn between an old friend and his wife—not a good position. He thought for sure coming here would help clear up any doubts he had or maybe Rick might confess something, but he felt exactly the same as when he walked in, confused.

"I think it would look better if you didn't hide from us. It makes you look more suspicious. And I can't promise Lily won't get off your case."

"Maybe you could put in a good word for me."

"I don't know if that's even possible."

Rick sighed. "You might think she has better instincts than anyone but she's human and is definitely wrong here."

"Unlikely. But I'll tell you what, if you stopped dating Marcia, I bet Lily would ease up."

"No chance. Marcia is integral to…my life."

James looked at him like he had three heads. "You just met her. How is that possible?"

Rick shifted in his seat, and then sucked down more

of his shake. "Our relationship moved fast, what can I say?" He set down his glass with a loud *clunk.* "Look man, you invited me to Manorview to help you out, now you're accusing me of taking advantage of a woman who happens to work for your wife. What is all this about anyway?"

James breathed in. He'd wanted to feel Rick out, but he hadn't expected to feel so unsettled. "I don't know what this is about. I'm as unsure as you are."

"Whatever it is, I think we should put it to rest. Lily's upset I made moves on her employee. That's all. Am I going to stop seeing Marcia? No. I don't think anyone should stand in our way. If you could smooth it over with the missus, I would be forever grateful."

Rick stood. "Thanks for the grub. I'm meeting up with some friends tonight and I need to get cleaned up. Let's do this again soon but remember I'm not the enemy." He walked out of the diner, confidence in his features as well as body language.

After Rick left, James let out the breath he'd been holding. The meeting hadn't gone the way he'd planned. He didn't know what Rick was up to and he had no evidence of any wrongdoing, but James recognized the familiar feeling creeping up from the depths of his bones.

The feeling was doubt.

****

Later that night, James realized from the meeting he'd had with Rick that he knew exactly where he should go next, Saint Nicholas Church. Even though James had previously spent a few hours outside the church looking for the recruiter with nothing to show for it, he realized he needed to put more of an effort.

Located in the center of town, the stone church stood

on an entire block of land surrounded by maple trees covered in red and yellow leaves, succumbing to the fall season. James parked in the small lot behind the church. Evening mass was about to begin, and James wanted to know if Sam—if that was his real name—had come out to recruit for the rituals.

Goosebumps dotted his arms as he approached the massive building. In the darkness, the gothic spires and opened-mouth gargoyles gave him the creeps. Lights on the inside of the sanctuary illuminated a religious scene portrayed in a stained-glass window. James had never been much of a religious man. His parents hadn't pushed him one way or another, so he chose to take the middle road. Did he believe there could be a higher power? Maybe. But this experience sure didn't help.

He slowly walked past a few well-dressed churchgoers and watched as a white-haired couple made it through the doors without being solicited by anyone with flyers. James melted into the shadows as more cars pulled into the lot. He figured a recruiter would want to target people before they went in and not after mass when they might likely feel more connected to their religion church. In the short time he'd lived in Manorview he'd learned most locals preferred going to this particular church, which meant a lot of them would be exposed to Sam the recruiter.

That made him wonder who Zeus's followers were. Any one of these people walking in could become a follower of the cult. He wanted to help them if he could. Catching Sam would lead him in the right direction. Heck, maybe Sam knew a lot more than James realized. Maybe he could get the exact location of the rituals out of him or even the truth behind its leader.

Patiently, he watched as several other couples walked in without issue. Had he been too optimistic? Had his growing suspicions of Rick steered him in the wrong direction? His phone buzzed in his pocket. Glancing at it, he saw Lily was calling but since he wasn't ready to admit his slight change of heart in this case, he didn't pick up. She'll be wondering where he was, so he'd have to decide sooner rather than later if he wanted to continue this charade. He looked at his watch, three minutes until the mass started and most of the attendees had already gone into the church. And then he saw a figure emerge from the corner of the entrance.

The person was lean and tall in a denim jacket and black boots. He was clearly masculine. This was it. Sam, the recruiter, stood only a few feet away. James watched as an elderly woman walked toward the door alone. Sam startled her at first but then she seemed pacified when he showed her a document he'd pulled out of his pocket. She took it in her hand. A few more words were exchanged that James couldn't hear and then she went inside. Sam had clearly handed her the Zeus flyer. This was his chance.

James began walking swiftly toward Sam. Once recognition appeared on Sam's face, he turned around in a full sprint.

"Stop! Police!" James yelled as he ran at full tilt.

But Sam kept running, crossing the street and onto the sidewalk up a steep hill. James's lungs burned as he pushed his legs even harder. Jumping over flower gardens and swiping tree branches away, James closed the gap between them. Taking a bold step, he launched himself at Sam, hoping to take him down to the ground in one leap.

"I didn't do anything," Sam cried out, struggling under James's body.

Putting his entire weight on Sam's back, James clasped the man's wrists in one hand while searching his pockets for weapons and more of the brochures. "I've got you now. You're not going to recruit anyone else to that sick cult."

"What? What sick cult?" Sam called out. "Man, I have no idea what you are talking about."

James showed him the document he'd pulled out of his denim jacket pocket. "This is what I'm talking about. How can you be part of something so disgusting?"

"Disgusting? It's just bingo night at the high school. I'm not recruiting anyone to a cult. I swear. You've got the wrong guy."

James's stomach dropped. He looked at the document.

Join Us for an Evening of Fun and Games: Bingo Night at Manorview High School

Even though the paper had been about the same size as the Zeus brochure, James had obviously been wrong. He cleared his throat and released the man's arms. This was not Sam.

"I was looking for someone in particular. A man who hands out flyers to try and recruit people into a cult. Know anyone who hangs out near the church by the name of Sam?"

The man stood and shook dirt from his jacket and pants. "No, never heard of him," he replied in a clipped tone. "I'll be sure to keep an eye out. Can I go now?"

"Yeah." James waved the man away. Then he stared at the bingo advertisement as the man jogged away in the other direction. Nausea roiled in his stomach as embarrassment set in.

The small shred of doubt Rick had left him with made him take chances he normally wouldn't take on a whim. And he'd been so frustrated with the holes in this case he'd clearly miscalculated.

But his boss, Abrams, did not need to know about this incident and neither did Lily. In fact, James would tell no one.

Chapter Thirteen

"That looks great." Rick leaned over Marcia to give a peck on the top of her head. "Good work."

"How many more do we need?" she asked from the small table near the kitchen that doubled as a dining table.

"I would keep going until you're tired. These brochures have really increased membership numbers. I'm so lucky to have met someone with so much artistic talent. The ones we had were looking pretty sad until you came along."

Marcia smiled at him as he made himself more comfortable on her beige worn-out couch. He knew she'd be flattered. Art was her passion. And that worked out very well for him. He reached over to grab the beer bottle on the side table and gulped down some cold brew. A burp erupted out of his mouth.

"Gross," she complained.

He smiled in her direction, although she had not looked up from her work.

"I'm happy to do this," she said. "I hope it pleases the gods and...you, of course."

Rick made his expression solemn. "Your contribution will not go unnoticed. Your idea to include the number twelve to pay homage to the twelve Gods of Olympus was very clever. I'm sure your hard work will help secure favorability in the eyes of the gods."

She placed another finished brochure in the growing pile next to her. "Tell me more about how you rose to your position and managed to find so many followers."

He watched her tuck a strand of mousy brown hair behind her ear. She wasn't particularly beautiful, and he certainly wasn't in love with her. He had bigger things to do. But if she knew *all* about him, she'd run for sure. "Marcia, everyone wants better fortune but so few are willing to go the extra mile. I'm simply providing a forum for people with similar desires to gather."

She blinked her large brown eyes. "But how did you know you were the one to do the teachings?"

Rick sighed and rubbed his bald head. *Too many questions.*

"My family taught me everything I needed to know." He took another swig of his beer, enjoying the burn down his throat. "All I did was listen. A little faith and hard work is all you need to convince people of your and their purpose. Everyone wants to belong to something. I simply provided a safe and common ground for them to gather and remember the ancients."

What she didn't know was how screwed up his past really was. His family had been involved in crime for as long as he could remember. A dabble in organized crime here, a little bit of fraud there but never on the right side of the law. He'd tried going straight. Heck, he'd become a cop, but his real nature had found its way out. He'd also been inspired by the case of the hospital worker who absconded with recently deceased persons in order to sell the organs. He thought that seemed like a great idea and has been eager to be a copycat. But he wouldn't tell Marcia about that part.

"*And* you're a detective. I'm such a lucky girl."

He got up to stand behind her and knead her shoulders. His massive body towered over her. "As long as you stick with me everything will be all right."

Marcia dropped her head back, enjoying the massage. "I think Lily has become suspicious. She might get in the way of our plans. I'm worried she'll fire me or catch on."

His hands stopped kneading. "We know she's suspicious but that's all. Has she done more than follow us around to dinner?"

Marcia looked down at the table. Her shoulders tensed up. "The other day she asked about us."

"Uh-huh." Rick's head pounded. The mere mention of Lily sticking her nose in his business changed his mood.

"She seemed to question what I see in you."

"Of course she did. She's obsessed with me. The minute I stepped into their place she began to follow me around. She knows nothing though and soon she and hubby will be on their honeymoon, out of our way."

"That will make it better." Marcia sighed. "I would love to go on a honeymoon." She looked up at him with twinkle-eyes.

He cleared his throat. "Maybe someday. For now, we need to focus on getting as many people to the gathering as we can to keep the funds flowing. For the next gathering, I'm going to charge more. It will be grander. More sacrifices. More fortune for everyone."

He sat back down on the couch. His heart raced when he got excited. If he was going to charge people more money, he'd have to give them something more to see. "But it means we'll have to give our followers more. It means we'll have to acquire more bodies." He watched for her reaction—not the typical request but if she bit he knew he'd succeeded in convincing her.

"That shouldn't be a problem." She didn't skip a beat. "I'll do anything to keep our family together. I thought the Reynolds Funeral Home was my family, but the Reynolds always come first in that place. And as long as you can keep Antonio happy with the bribes, we should be able to continue sneaking out of the garage undetected."

Rick smiled. He knew he was good but not this good. "That's why we've got to keep the fees rolling in. It's not cheap installing those church-boy decoys to keep suspicion low."

She looked up from her work. "What decoys?"

"The boys I hired to hand out bingo night flyers whenever they spot the cops pull up—keeps our recruiters from getting caught."

"Oh, and you throw the bingo night party, too?"

He shook his head. "If anyone shows up for it they'll think it got canceled."

"Got it. That is elaborate."

"And expensive but I know you will do anything for us which also means keeping Lily off your case. If she keeps on pursuing us our family will be torn apart. And the gods will surely be upset."

"Of course. I would never want to upset the gods or you. Lily will never know our secret."

Rick blew out the air he'd been holding. Without Marcia he couldn't possibly get everything done the right way. He needed her almost as much as she needed him. He couldn't believe how lucky he'd been. It had all been too easy.

Soon after arriving at the funeral home he'd

identified Marcia as the weakest link among them. He had been like a magnet to her timid nature, and he knew she would be a pawn in his game, but also a very important one.

Zachary, on the other hand, had not succumbed so easily. A few trips to Old Town Bar had loosened his tongue enough for Rick to learn about the kid's insecurities. Deep-seated issues regarding his parents' death bubbled to the surface after two drinks. He talked about the mistakes he'd made in the past and his trouble with the law. Rick knew Zachary was searching for some stability and he would gladly provide it in exchange for his trust. It all seemed almost too easy—except for Lily. He sighed.

"What's wrong?" she asked.

"Nothing. I was just thinking about how we met and how grateful I am."

She smiled. "I'm glad you were curious about my casket art that day. Even though I noticed you, I never would've started the conversation."

"It's not every day one sees a phoenix rising from the ashes painted on someone's casket."

She giggled. "That was Mr. Parker. His family said that's what he would have wanted because he loved the idea of transformation."

"And it brought us together to do great things."

"When will you write the new sermon? I'm almost done with the new brochures for the next meeting."

"It's already written." He pointed to his head. "It's all in here."

Chapter Fourteen

Sitting in her office, Lily typed *Rubin Mansion, Manorview, NY* into the search bar on her computer screen. She needed to find its exact location and anything else noteworthy. The first link she clicked on took her to the real estate transaction between the previous owner and its most recent one. The mansion, located on Sunshine Lane, had been sold to Dr. George Rubin for seven million dollars twelve years ago.

"Knock. Knock." Shanna poked her head into the office. "I'm all set with Mr. Tang's embalming." She looked at her watch. "Ready to go?"

Distracted, Lily looked up. "What are we doing again?"

Shanna's glare brought her back to reality. "Oh, right. Dress shopping. I'll be right there," she promised and went back to staring at the screen.

Shanna walked into the office and sat in the chair opposite Lily's desk. "What are you up to now?"

"Research on the Rubin mansion."

Shanna scrunched up her face. "Rubin mansion? Why that place?"

"I have some theories I need to suss out."

"Understood. The Rubins were quite flashy from what I heard."

Lily peered at her from behind the screen. "What do you mean?"

"I think Dr. Rubin overextended himself financially, probably to impress his third wife," Shanna said and continued. "They drove expensive cars and traveled the world but eventually the money ran out."

"Did they have any kids?"

"No. Word on the street has it one day they just walked out of that place and never looked back. It went up for auction, but no one seemed interested. I haven't seen the place myself, but I heard the stone is crumbling bit by bit."

"Sad," Lily mumbled. "Now it's being used for something else."

"What something else?"

"Nothing. I don't want to involve you unless I absolutely need to. I want you to enjoy your engagement."

"Mighty thoughtful of you but I still work here and if it has to do with all the body snatching, I have the right to know."

Lily sat back in her chair. "I might know who's to blame."

Shanna leaned forward. "You do?"

"But I'm not quite there yet. I need more time."

Shanna pursed her lips. "You're not going to tell your own sister?"

"Not yet but soon." Lily glanced at the time. "We should go. We're going to be late for your appointment with Madam Tulle."

"Fine." Shanna rose from her chair. "I'll wait in the car. Don't take too long. Believe it or not it takes forever to get an appointment there." She rose and made her way to the door.

"I believe it. Remember, I did this not too long ago

and almost lost my mind."

Shanna smiled. "I never pegged you as a bridezilla, but it happens to the best of us."

"Har, har. If that were my only issue, I'd be thrilled. Oh, and I've made some headway on our Reynolds Royal Weddings venture."

"And?"

"You're skeptical but the website is up, and I've already got some client appointments lined up."

Shanna's eyebrows shot up. "Wow. I am impressed. I never thought this would catch on. We may be used to this type of atmosphere and willing to get married amongst the deceased, but I didn't think other people would."

"There's probably a uniqueness to it that people want to explore—something different than your average venue."

"I guess. Let me know if you need help. You've got a lot going on with the honeymoon looming, my wedding to plan, a new business venture, your regular job, and a criminal investigation."

Lily frowned. "Don't remind me."

After Shanna proceeded toward the car, Lily took another minute to tidy up her desk and shut down her computer. She grabbed her purse, digging into its side pouch where she kept her face powder. A little dab on her forehead, nose, other shiny bits and she was on her way. Down she went toward garage where her car was parked. Getting new tires had been expensive and time consuming. She wanted to hand the bill over to Rick but reconsidered when she realized that might not go over well with James.

As she passed the entrance to the basement, she

heard Zachary talking to someone but couldn't make out the words. Unable to contain her nosiness, Lily leaned into the entrance of the basement.

"Huh?" She heard him say out loud.

She sighed knowing from experience this couldn't be good sign. Reluctantly, she walked down the stairs. "Zachary?"

His expression seemed perplexed as he stared at the refrigerators.

Dread overcame her body. "Something wrong?" She glanced at Shanna who must've become impatient sitting in the car and had walked down the short set of steps from the garage into the basement.

"Uh. I can't seem to find Ms. Knight or Mr. Weiner. I swear I put them both in here last night." He opened the latch to one of the horizontal compartments and pulled its door open. "It's empty." He said, shrugging his shoulders. "And so is the other."

Lily's chest burned. She couldn't believe it; she didn't *want* to believe it. She pointed at Shanna. "Tell me this is a sick joke, Zachary. Tell me you two are pulling a prank."

"I wish, but I checked all the compartments. They're not here."

"Oh for the love—" Lily pinched the bridge of her nose as she paced the room.

"Is this really happening?" Shanna asked.

"Yep, two more bodies are gone," Lily snapped. "It seems Zachary doesn't quite remember what happened to them."

Shanna glared at their brother. "What do you mean you don't remember? Were you drinking?"

"No. Stop both of you." Zachary's hands went up in

defense. "I know I put them in here last night. I just came to check on them and they're gone."

"Again?" Shanna yelped.

"Zach, I've got to be honest," Lily said. "It looks a little suspicious. Are you sure you didn't have anything to do with it?"

"Of course not. How would I be involved?"

"You seem mighty friendly with Rick lately. I wonder if he's gotten to you, too."

Zachary scrunched up his face. "I have no idea what you're talking about. *You* sound like the crazy one with all your conspiracy theories."

"All right. Let's calm down." Shanna squeezed Lily's arm. "Should we call the cops?"

"No," Lily snapped.

"*No*? Why not?" Shanna asked.

"Because it won't make a difference. They're already investigating the other two missing bodies, what's two more?"

"Losing faith in your investigators?" Shanna smiled.

"Yes, I am. We all know the only person who's going to catch the body snatcher is me." She pointed to her chest. "So Shanna, let's get in the car and go look at some brides' dresses. Zachary, I swear if you know something and aren't telling me there will be hell to pay." She walked up the steps into the garage.

His arm went out in surrender. "I don't know anything. Rick's been a good friend."

"We'll see about that." She slammed the outer door.

"Aren't you being a little rough on him?" Shanna asked as she got into the car.

Lily also got in and turned on the engine. "I feel like everyone is lying to me."

"You really *are* a detective."

"In the past I would've loved to hear you say that."

"And now?"

"Not so much."

Chapter Fifteen

"Thanks for coming, man," Zachary said as Rick playfully slapped him on the back.

"I'm always here for you." Rick sat at the bar and had to wonder why so many people ended up at Old Town Bar. The stench reminded him of old socks soaked in beer. But then again, there weren't too many options in Manorview—a far cry from the endless options in The City.

"I ordered that brown ale you like." Zachary lifted his beer glass. "Cheers."

Rick grabbed his glass. "To friendship. May you always have someone to lean on."

Zachary smiled and clicked his glass with Rick's. "Is that someone, you?"

"Of course. Who else is going to give you bad relationship advice?"

"You're a little too late. Julie and I broke up."

Rick's smile faded. "Seriously? Aww man, I'm sorry. When did that happen?"

"A couple weeks ago. She said she didn't think I'm mature enough for her."

"You're both young. How can either of you be mature?"

"I think she never got over my attempted murder."

Rick took a step back. The more Rick got to know Zach the more he was reminded of his own youth. "Care to explain?"

"Last year an employee named Simon from a rival funeral home tried to kill me. I was stabbed a bunch of times, but I survived. Julie had to help me recover." Zachary pulled down the collar of his T-shirt revealing a long scar below his clavicle. "I don't think she wants to deal with that ever again."

"Geez, is that place still in business?"

Rick took a long gulp of his beer. He felt like he was talking to one of his old buddies before attempting the honest life. The type of trouble those guys used to get into would make anyone's hair stand up—but not him. To Rick, it felt natural.

Zachary chuckled. "No, stabbing people is an automatic fail. Simon and the owner, Tina, were arrested. The place was shut down. Oh, and incidentally, Marcia and Chris used to work for that rival home. Lily felt bad after it went down the toilet and hired them."

Rick's ears perked up. No wonder Marcia had been an easy sell. She must have had instincts toward the dark side if she had been previously working for a criminal. "Interesting. Sometimes people have good intentions but don't know how to execute them properly. It depends."

"On what?" Zachary's voice went up an octave.

"On the stakes. Look, I'm not saying they should have stabbed you, but they clearly wanted to protect something important."

"Yeah, they were protecting the wacko owner. That doesn't make it right."

"I'm trying to help you cope that's all." Rick sensed he could manipulate Zachary as long as he continued to have his back. The kid had deep-seated abandonment issues that could be easily exploited.

Zachary inhaled half his beer. "Then you need to talk to Julie because clearly *she* did not cope well."

"I can if you want me to. It must all be a misunderstanding. What are the chances that your funeral home goes under attack again?"

"Pretty slim."

"I'd agree. So what is Julie so worried about? I can talk to her if you'd like."

"I appreciate that, but I think Lily might get upset. Besides, we have had a couple hiccups lately with bodies going missing. Two went missing the other day—taken right from under our noses. I swear they're disappearing into thin air."

Rick sucked in a breath. He'd known this would probably come up. Eventually he hoped he get close enough to Zachary to recruit him into stealing more. But for now he'd play it off. "That is odd. Maybe you have a burglar selling bodies. I thought James had the place locked up tight?"

"Sort of. Nobody has seen anyone or anything out of the ordinary. Between you and me," Zachary lowered his voice, "Lily thinks you might have something to do with it."

Rick chuckled. "Of course she does. I'm an outsider. It's easy to pick on me."

"I think she's lost it."

"Maybe, like I said before, it depends on the stakes. Lily places a high value on her business so she means to protect it at any cost. Even if there's no proof or logic behind her accusations." Rick tapped Zachary's shoulder. "I'm sure you can put in a good word for your big brother."

Zachary smiled. "It must be a misunderstanding.

Lily's good at what she does but she ain't perfect." He shrugged. "Why would she go down this road with you?"

Rick shook his head. "You got me." He pointed his index finger up in the air. "Although, I think she might be upset I took Marcia on a date."

Zachary grinned. "You took Marcia out on a date? You dirty dog."

Rick's arms went out in defense. "Hey! I can't help it if she finds me irresistible."

Zachary drank his beer while a frown developed between his brows. "Well, she didn't approach you, that's for sure."

"Listen, I happen to like art and she's an artist. We are a match made in heaven."

Zachary scrunched up his face. "I don't know about that. She's pretty quiet compared to you. It's more like a surprising match."

"You told me Julie likes to go to rodeos whenever she has time. I know you don't like rodeos, but you dated her anyway."

"Different. Going to rodeos is a hobby, not a personality trait."

"Haven't you heard of opposites attract?" Rick threw his head back and finished his beer in one gulp.

"It doesn't matter. If you like each other, I'm happy for you. And you're probably right; Lily wouldn't like to see you two together. She's protective of her staff even if they came from a rival funeral home."

"Well, that explains why she would pin some crazy body snatcher on me. Everyone has their flaws, but I want you to remember I'm here for you even if your family members falsely accuse me of crimes I didn't commit. I'm not going anywhere."

Rick knew that's what Zachary wanted. As long as he can keep Zachary and Marcia on his side he should be in the clear. How persistent could Lily really be? He had a feeling he might find out. "Any girls in here catch your eye?" He looked around at the girl groups sitting at the bar. "I could be your wingman."

"Highly unlikely in this dump. Besides, I'm not ready yet."

"That's cool. Like I said I'll be here when you're ready." Rick eyed the phone in Zach's hand. The home screen had not locked yet. He reached over and snatched the phone out of Zachary's hand.

"Hey!"

"I just want to see something." Rick began furiously searching Zach's contact list. And because he was significantly taller than Zachary, he could keep the phone away long enough to make a call. "Hello, Julie?"

"What are you doing?" Zachary complained as he reached for the phone.

But Rick dodged and arched his body away from Zachary's reach. "My name is Rick. I'm a friend of Zachary Reynolds. We're having a drink at Old Town Bar catching up when he told me he misses you."

Zachary put his hands over his ears and closed his eyes.

"You miss him, too? Well, I think you should come by and have a drink. It can't hurt to have a conversation. Oh great, you're on your way. We'll be here waiting." Rick tapped the screen to end the call. His eyes were wide. "I didn't think that would work. But it did."

Zachary snatched his phone back. "What have you done?"

"I took a chance. It paid off." He shrugged his

shoulders. "You can't be mad when it pays off."

Zachary took a breath. "Holy cow. I can't believe that worked. I can't decide if I should be mad or happy."

Rick slapped Zachary's back. "Be happy, man. This is your chance and clearly, she misses you, too."

Zachary motioned at the bartender for another round. "I'm in shock."

"You'll be fine. Here's your chance to explain to her that you've grown a lot and you're extremely responsible—even though you did nothing wrong. If you want her back, you'll need to play the game. I'm sure she feels like she made a mistake, or else why would she be coming here?"

"True. I hope this wasn't a bad idea."

"Nah, it's genius. Drink up."

Ten minutes later, Rick noticed a tall brunette walk into the bar. She paused at the door scanning the patrons.

"Julie," Zachary announced and waved her over.

She smiled and headed toward the bar. As she walked her brown hair bounced on her shoulders.

Rick watched Zachary's smile spread from ear to ear. This was not just a great idea. It was brilliant. "Hey, I'm Rick. I talked to you on the phone earlier."

Julie smiled. "I figured. Nice to meet you, Rick."

Rick put his hand over his chest. "Sorry for the imposition but he talks about you, so I did what I thought was right."

Zachary rolled his eyes. "I ordered the beer you like. He handed her the bottle.

"Thanks. I just finished a clinical rotation so I could use a drink."

"Julie is in nursing school," Zachary explained.

"A noble profession." Rick said. "When do you

graduate?"

"This coming spring. I'm not sure I'm ready though."

"You'll be great," Zachary said. "You'd be great at anything you chose."

Rick threw his head back to drink the last few drops of his beer. Then he placed the empty bottle on the bar. His gamble had paid off. Sometimes he couldn't believe how easily he could manipulate people. With Zachary on his side it would be hard for Lily to convince him that Rick had been anything but an upstanding fellow.

"Well, my work is done here. I'll let you two get reacquainted."

Zachary stood up. "Thanks for everything, man. You're the best."

"Anytime. I'm here for you." Rick walked to the front door. Then he turned around. "Remember that," he said before he walked out.

Chapter Sixteen

By appointment only, Madame Tulle's was Manorview's only store that sold wedding attire. Racks and racks of bridal dresses lined the walls in every shape and texture possible. A handful of brides-to-be sifted through poufy princess dresses with big smiles on their faces. Lily remembered that feeling, although her dress has been...more manageable. Then she noticed the slimmer beaded options on a separate rack.

"You like shiny things." Lily pointed. "Why don't you start there?"

"Maybe I will." Shanna gestured toward the section of colorful bridesmaids dresses. "And you should look over there."

Lily's eyes narrowed. "Right. What color did you say we were wearing?"

"Blush. I thought it would look nice for spring."

Lily nodded and made her way to the bridesmaid's section as the sales associate came out to greet them. "Good day, ladies, my name is Ramona. Please let me know how I can be of assistance."

Lily turned to her. Ramona's glasses sat halfway down her nose with a beaded cord that swung and hit her jaw as she moved her head. "I'm all set, but I think the bride over there might need some help."

As Ramona moved in Shanna's direction, Lily turned to the bridesmaid dresses, barely able to focus.

With two more missing bodies, and a possible location for the rituals, looking into any of these dresses seemed low on the totem pole of importance.

"Lily," Shanna called.

Lily turned to find her sister holding out a fitted strapless satin gown with beads running up and down the entire length of the dress. The back was open with a lace train cascading down for one foot past the hem of the dress. "Look at this."

"It's beautiful," Lily said.

"Isn't it?" Ramona said with her hands clasped together. "The cut will be perfect for you,"

Shanna smiled. "I'm going to try it on." She rushed off toward the fitting room while Lily grabbed the simplest chiffon blush gown she could find and waited on the velvet couch for Shanna to emerge.

"Would you like some champagne?" Ramona asked.

"No, thank you."

"Great choice," she added, pointing to the blush-colored dress in Lily's hand.

Lily's jaw dropped when Shanna stepped out of the dressing room. "Wow. You look beautiful."

Shanna smiled as she stared at herself in the mirror. Her eyes glittered with excitement. "Do I need to try more?"

Lily got up and stood beside her in front of the mirror. "Probably would be smart. But it does fit you perfectly."

Ramona approached Shanna with a glass of champagne. "It looks fabulous," she crooned. "I'll start pulling the veils."

Shanna took the glass. "Great. You don't want

any?" she asked, turning toward Lily.

Lily shook her head. "No, you enjoy it."

"Don't feel like celebrating?" She sipped the champagne.

"I do. I'm happy for you. You look amazing." Lily shrugged. "Do I feel bad about yelling at Zachary? A little and maybe I have too much going on."

"You were hard on him. He has nothing to do with this mess."

Lily nodded. "You're right. I think I secretly resent that he's gotten so close to a horrible person. But I get why it's happened."

"You're under a lot of stress. But I do think you should talk to him."

"I will."

Ramona appeared at Shanna's side. "I think this hip-length veil with lace edges would suit you perfectly." She placed the clip into Shanna's blonde hair.

"That is really pretty," Shanna said, smiling wide as she arched her body to see more of the veil as it fell down her back.

Lily hadn't seen her sister this happy in a long time. "It is beautiful. Are the other bridesmaids having a fitting?"

"Later this week. Since you're the matron of honor, I thought you should get first choice on the style of dress. The one you picked looks great." Shanna took another sip of her champagne.

"Have you thought about your bachelorette party?" Lily asked.

"No, have you?" Shanna eyed her sister with suspicion.

Lily's shoulders went up. "What? A night out at Old

Town Bar isn't sufficient?"

Shanna rolled her eyes.

"Followed by a ghost tour of Manorview?"

Her face scrunched up. "Is there such a thing?"

"There should be. With all the strange stuff we see, why wouldn't there be creepy stuff going on?"

"Is that your next business venture?"

Lily smiled. "Now you're talking." She lifted up her dress. "Do I have to try this on?"

"Yup." Shanna finished her champagne.

"Fine." Lily walked toward the dressing room. "Don't drink the whole bottle while I'm in there."

"Why not?"

She winked at her sister. "I won't be able to trust your opinion when I come out in this dress."

"You won't trust my opinion anyway."

"True." Lily made her way into the dressing room, which didn't disappoint with its simple but elegant furniture and large mirror up against the wall. The pink and white potted orchid on a small table near the mirror was a nice touch.

Wasting no time, she stripped off her black cardigan, beige mock tee and dark blue jeans. The sudden change in temperature made goose bumps appear on her skin. She quickly shimmied into the long chiffon blush dress and tied the thin belt around her waist, cinching the dress to her curves. The straight cut fit seamlessly on her lean torso. The blush color complemented her long fiery locks and silver-grey eyes.

"Looks great," Shanna said, entering the dressing room without knocking.

"Not bad." Lily turned her body to see more angles in the mirror.

"You'll make a perfect matron of honor."

Lily smiled at Shanna in the mirror. "You'll make a great wife. Just make sure Abrams stays out of my way."

"He wouldn't dream of getting involved. Don't forget he eventually came around to support you."

"He was also the one who accused me of murdering Michael Ronan."

"It's all water under the bridge." Shanna squeezed Lily's waist. "We're all one big happy family now."

"I would've said dysfunctional."

Shanna nodded. "That, too."

"Come on, let's go wrap this up so I can go stalk an abandoned building in the woods and look for my body snatcher."

"All right, but shouldn't we look at more dress options?"

Lily looked at Shanna's dress up and down. "Nah, I think this is the one. Unless you want to drive into The City and look for more."

"Ugh, no thanks. I think you're right, this is the one." Shanna scooped up the train in her arms. "I wish Mom and Dad were here to see this."

Lily grabbed her hand. "I do, too. Mom's probably dying to weigh in on the dress and Dad's probably thinking, *she's finally getting married.*"

Shanna laughed. "Sounds about right. Anyway, I'm glad you're here and I'm sure they're happy about that."

"Definitely, although I bet they are both huffing and puffing over the bodies we lost." Lily noticed a bit of shock on Ramona's face. She'd been so caught up in her problems she'd forgotten how people reacted to all things related to funeral homes.

Shanna crossed her arms. "And I'm not sure they

would love the idea of hosting weddings at the funeral home either."

"Oh, I don't know. I think it celebrates the funeral home instead of it always being a place no one wants to visit."

Shanna's voice fell. "True."

"What's the matter?" Lily asked.

"I just miss them. I wish they could be here to see all our accomplishments."

Lily rubbed Shanna's arm. "I'm one hundred percent sure they are here."

Chapter Seventeen

"I know James has been snooping around in my business," Chris Tuchman said, closing the door after he entered Lily's office. "I know why he's doing it, but I can't.say it's making me happy."

"Have a seat." Lily gestured to the visitor's chair and folded her arms on the table. "It's been crazy here. I don't have to tell you that. As you know two more bodies were stolen and truthfully, we have been unable to discover anything helpful on the case, which explains why James has been looking to investigate everyone. You've been really helpful and a great manager. But when James gets something in his head, he runs with it until the end, no matter the cost."

She saw a preoccupied look in Chris's eyes. He returned a small smile. "I know the minute something weird happens in here all eyes look to me and Marcia. That's the risk we took in working here but I didn't expect *this*."

"How did you know James was looking around?"

"Stan, my roommate told me—that jerk. He's the one making up stuff about me."

"Why would he do that?"

"He's mad because he thinks I stole his girl, which is not true. She never liked him in the first place."

"Slim pickings in Manorview, huh?"

"You're not wrong there. I'm close to finishing my

undergraduate degree, then I'll apply to business school. Maybe then, I'll move out of this town."

"Probably a good idea. You don't want to get stuck here with all of your talents, although, I would hate to lose you. I'm sorry if James offended you but you're not under investigation."

Chris let out a breath. "That's good to know. I hate the idea of being investigated when I did nothing wrong."

"Understood. I assure you it's likely a formality and not much else. Can we move past this?"

He waved his hand. "I'm already over it."

"Great, because I have a proposition for you."

Chris's right eyebrow rose. "I'm listening."

Lily returned a mischievous grin. "I've opened up the funeral home to weddings and I thought it would be perfect if you officiated them." She said it before he could take another breath.

But he sat frozen for a minute.

She continued. "I don't expect this is an option for everyone, but weddings are expensive, and it won't look like a funeral home after we decorate it. The coffin sales room would be closed, and people wouldn't have access to any area that might resemble a funeral home."

Lily waited for his reaction. She hoped he wasn't about to quit. Trying to find a new manager on top of everything might send her to the looney bin.

"Or maybe they do want to see the coffins. That could be why they booked the wedding in the first place."

Lily laughed, releasing the built-up tension. She knew Chris wasn't that easy to spook. "Maybe. I guess we'll find out sooner rather than later. Will you do it?"

"Why not? I already work in a funeral home. This actually seems more straight forward."

"Perfect. I've got a couple coming over today who are interested in having their wedding here. I might have you meet them."

He nodded. "All right."

"Incidentally, how *did* you get into the funeral home business? It doesn't seem like the first choice for a young man."

"Isn't that how most people get into unexpected job choices? I needed a job and Innovations Funeral Home was hiring. As you know, I had management experience in retail. If one can handle that, they can handle a lot."

Lily nodded. "Agreed. And I bet there wasn't too much competition for your job at Innovations."

"It turned out I'm pretty good at what I do."

"Yes, you are the best."

Chris opened his notepad and grabbed the pen from his front jacket pocket. He clicked the top of the pen. "Where is our lovely couple from?"

"Brooklyn, New York. Sandy Goodwill and Jack Wright. I know Jack works in graphics; I think Sandy's an educator."

He smiled as he jotted down their names. "It's impressive that you attracted people from The City to our humble little town."

"That seems to be the pattern around here," she grumbled.

"What?"

"I was referring to our guest, Rick. He's also from The City and a friend of James. Has he been getting in your way at all?"

Chris closed his notepad. "No, James introduced

me. He seems like a charming fellow."

"Ha! Charming for sure." She leaned forward. "He's dating Marcia."

Chris's jaw dropped. "Deer-in-headlights Marcia?"

"The same one." Lily sat back on her chair. "I don't like it."

"I'll bet. The last thing we need is a broken-hearted make-up artist. Or who knows maybe they'll be together forever."

"I doubt it." Lily sucked in a breath. "Do me a favor. Keep an eye on them for me."

"Fine. But this is well beyond my job description."

"Understood. What would I do without you?"

He grinned. "That same thing you always do, Lily, succeed."

****

Lily eyed the couple sitting across from her desk. Sandy Goodwill rocked her jet-black hairstyle with blunt-cut bangs. She wore a cobalt blue dress with black tights and Mary Jane shoes. Her fiancé, Jack Wright, had chin-length frizzy brown hair and round glasses. He wore black and white striped pants and brown shoes. Lily had wondered who her target audience would be for a funeral wedding venue, and with these two she wasn't disappointed. And at least the body snatcher wouldn't be interested in them since they weren't departing with a body today.

"Our parents don't approve but we think the grounds and space are amazing for a wedding. From the website I could tell you keep everything so well maintained," Sandy said. "The willow trees along the sides of the house are so beautiful."

"They are, especially in the springtime. Would you

be interested in a spring wedding?"

The couple smiled at each other. "That sounds perfect."

"I can assure you it will not feel like a funeral home on the day of your wedding. The main viewing room will be where the reception will be held. It will be decorated with the flowers of your choice, which I understand from your application to be orange-colored roses with white linen tables and a live band."

Sandy reached over to give Jack's hand a squeeze. "Yes."

"The coffin sales room will be converted into an open space for the cocktail hour with *hors d'oeuvres* and your choice of beverages."

As she explained the layout, Lily's eyes flickered to her silent ringing phone. Zachary was calling. She ignored it. "Of course the coffins will be removed."

The couple smiled in relief.

"It will not resemble a funeral home at all; I know your parents will be pleased. We have to iron out the catering options for the reception but other than a few more details we are on track for a spring wedding. The calendar is filling up so I'm glad you reached out to us when you did."

A second call came in from Zachary. His persistence probably had something to do with their last argument.

"I'm glad we reached out, too," Sandy said. "It all sounds great and well-organized."

Jack glanced at Sandy. "We hate to bring this up, but we'd heard about some strange activity here and we wanted some clarification before committing to having our wedding here. If you don't mind."

Lily's head pounded. "Strange activity?"

"We've heard some of your...clients have gone missing? Normally, we wouldn't listen to rumors but if there's an ongoing investigation, we don't want that to have an effect on our day."

Lily nodded, unsure of how to proceed. "In the interests of full disclosure, we have had a couple of incidents where our clients have been taken. We know who the culprit is and will be handing him over to authorities soon. In my mind the case is closed. Incidentally, who told you this information?"

"My aunt Milly lives in Manorview." Sandy interjected. "She brought it up, but we weren't sure what to make of the rumor."

Aunt Milly? Sounds like the rumors are coming from the local knitting crowd. Her staff had been warned not to talk about business issues with their families, but she realized that was an unrealistic expectation.

Jack remained expressionless. "What happens if the authorities decide to close down your business while it's under investigation? If that happens, we'd have to find a whole new venue in a short period of time."

"I understand your concern. Luckily, I work very closely with the investigators, and I know for a fact they are not going to shut my business down."

Jack and Sandy smiled in unison. It was the truth. They can shut her business down over *her* dead body.

"That's reassuring."

"Wonderful, let me give you a copy of your contract to read over and we can go from there."

Lily made her way to the printer. Reynolds Royal Weddings had its first client—hopefully—and she couldn't be more thrilled. Was she spreading herself a bit thin? Yes, but she wanted to pursue new opportunities as they appeared. And who knows, maybe the wedding business outperforms the funeral business? Her parents would roll over in their graves. Or maybe they would applaud her business savvy. Either way she would try as hard as possible to make it all work.

"Here you go." She handed the couple a copy of the contract. "Let's schedule a food tasting in the meantime. The Modern Kitchen has the best options for weddings. They can make delicious filet mignon or brown butter ravioli if you don't want meat."

"It's good to have a veggie option," Sandy said.

"Very true. And Modern Kitchen does have exceptional quality in all their food options." Lily looked at the calendar on her computer screen. "Let's set up the tasting for three weeks from now as a placeholder while you review the contract."

"Perfect. We are so thrilled this worked out."

"I am, too." Lily smiled at them. Boy, did she have to make this an amazing experience for them, and get Rick out of her life before he really screwed things up. She was up for the challenge.

After the excited couple left, Lily went to the embalming room to look for Shanna.

"Have you seen Zachary?" she asked as she put on a surgical mask.

Shanna, gowned up and also wearing a mask, poured embalming fluid into the machine used to pump the fluid into their clients arteries. "He's in the kitchen." She looked up from her task. "Feeling a little guilty about the other day?"

Lily sighed. "I need him to realize what is going on here. There are no playdates with strangers. This is serious."

"Oh, stop being so mean."

"He'll understand, right?"

"That he'll need to give up his only male role model and friend because his big sister thinks that same role model is a criminal?" She put her hand on her chest. "I certainly would understand but I'm not him."

"Ha! Very funny. I just got done meeting with our first wedding couple."

Shanna looked up from her task. "And?"

"They are super interested. But they did hear rumors about our body count situation."

"Oh, boy. I bet you weren't pleased."

Lily shook her head. "No, I was not happy. They were worried the funeral home would get shut down by an investigation."

"Ha! Over your dead body."

"That's what I said but I need to get this case solved before it ruins all my plans."

Shanna nodded.

"I'm going to find Zachary." Lily turned to leave. "Wish me luck."

"Good luck!" Shanna announced as she went back to filling the embalming machine.

Lily made her way toward the kitchen and found her brother eating mac and cheese out of a microwave container. "You called me?"

"I did. I wanted to talk to you about Rick," Zach said as he shoveled another spoonful of mac and cheese in his mouth.

Lily's insides burned. She pulled a chair out and sat across from him. She needed to be more delicate this time—for his sake and for hers as well. He might know something about Rick that he's been holding back.

"I'm listening."

He swallowed. "First of all, I had nothing to do with the missing bodies. For you to even think—"

She put up her hand. "Don't even worry about that. I never thought *you* did anything."

"Really? You seemed to insinuate—"

"I was wrong to make you feel that way. I don't know what I was thinking. I'm sorry."

Zachary's shoulders relaxed as if relinquishing whatever fight he had been prepared to undertake. "I'm glad you don't think I'm involved but you do think Rick has something to do with the missing bodies."

Lily nodded. "I'm pretty convinced he is involved but you can't tell him about this conversation."

Zachary got quiet.

She knew this was hard for him. He'd formed a relationship with Rick—albeit a false one. But her brother believed the man was being genuine.

"Rick is not who you think he is. He's infiltrated our family and has clearly gotten to you. I get that you like him. He's filling a hole in your life. We lost Dad when we were young; Rick has filled that role for you. But I assure you it's not real. It's an act to get you on his side."

Zachary scrunched up his face. "Why? What does he want?"

"I think he's involved in a body snatching scheme."

"But why? Why is he doing it?"

"I don't know. Crooked cop issues? Money? I want you to know what's going on and stay away from him. He's dangerous."

Zachary's blue eyes stared at the ground like he'd lost a puppy. "Is there any chance you could be wrong on this one?"

Lily sighed. "For your sake, I wish I was wrong. He's even got Marcia in the mix. She's convinced he's the greatest thing that's ever happened to her, not unlike yourself. That's how manipulative he is. I've tried to talk sense into her too, but she refuses to stop seeing him. You, on the other hand, should be hanging around James more often. You could do a boys' night with him and Abrams."

Zachary frowned. "Now *you're* the crazy one. Abrams is like a hundred years old. What do I have in common with him?"

Lily laughed. "He might be one hundred years old but I'm sure you could learn something from him."

"Like what? How to play vinyl records? If anything I would be teaching him how technology works these days."

"Well, that's something. He might like that. And there's nothing wrong with having a vinyl collection. He also has a samurai sword collection. You might find that history interesting."

Zachary's eyes glazed over.

"In any case, I'm sorry I yelled at you. This is a stressful case, and I wasn't expecting the enemy to be so close."

"It's cool. I trust your opinion, although I'm not totally sure about your theory. You're accusing someone I consider a friend."

"I know I'm making serious accusations, but I know I'm right. If you keep hanging out with Rick, I'm not sure I can protect you from him. I'm trying to get to you before it's too late."

Zachary breathed in. He seemed slightly annoyed but taking it all in. "I'll consider it. It's so hard to believe.

You know he helped me get back together with Julie."

"What? You're back with Julie?"

"Yeah, him and I were hanging at Old Town Bar when I told him how we'd broken up. He took a chance and called her, and it paid off. She came out to meet us."

"I'm not that surprised he did that. He took a gamble and it worked out, but you do see how he's trying to get you to love him, don't you? That's his MO."

He sighed again as if his soul was being torn off into pieces bit by bit. "I have the worst luck."

"No, you don't. You got Julie back and my warning makes you extremely lucky. Zachary, we have a criminal on our hands and he's jeopardizing our future here. So let's get real and save ourselves from disaster."

"Fine." He sat up and cleared his throat. "What do you need me to do?"

"Keep your eyes peeled, stay out of trouble, and tell me if you see something funny."

"Roger that." He saluted. "And Lily, don't worry, I'm not that damaged. Although, I think you might be."

Lily chuckled. Better to laugh than cry. "I think you might be right."

"So, what *are* you going to do about it?"

"Be patient. I've got a plan."

Chapter Eighteen

"The Rubin mansion?"

James jumped at Abrams's question. "Geez, sneaking up on me now?"

"You don't need to look up anything. I'm old as dirt and I happen to know everything about Manorview." Abrams walked over and sat in one of the chairs opposite James. "I remember a month wouldn't go by before we were called out to the Rubin mansion mostly for noise disturbances, which—given the size of the place—is saying a lot. That guy liked to party." Abrams scratched his temple. "If I'm not mistaken, he ended up in financial troubles and lost the place."

James nodded. "That's what I read in some old news articles."

"What's the catch?"

He knew he was going to sound crazy—not what he wanted to portray to his boss. "Lily thinks the body snatcher is holding rituals at the mansion."

Abrams's eyebrows shot up. "The same rituals you mentioned before?"

"Yep. Sacrificial, except the victims are already deceased."

Abrams's eyes darted back and forth. "Not much of a sacrifice. Seems like a flawed ritual. People will want their money back."

"You're hysterical," James replied with a dry tone.

"She also thinks the head guy is my buddy, Rick."

Abrams leaned forward. "Did I hear that right? The body snatcher is a friend of yours?"

"That's her theory, not mine. He's supposed to be house sitting while we go on our honeymoon."

Abrams leaned in closer. "The perp is living with you?"

James rubbed his chin. "It's messy."

"I would stay out of it. You have too many conflicts of interest."

"How can I stay out of it? My wife believes a friend of mine is threatening her business. She won't stop until the end."

"And what will be the end? All the bodies will go missing? And after he's used them all up will he go to the living for more supply?"

James threw his hands up in the air. "How is this helpful? Are you saying do nothing?"

Abrams sighed. "No, I'm hardwired to think of the worst-case scenario."

James held his head. "I can't believe Rick would do anything like that."

"If he did, I'll tell you one thing. Your friend has got some issues."

"Thanks, Captain Obvious."

Abrams nodded. "You're welcome but it must be the money. That's the only rational motive I can think of unless you think he's gone off the rails. I've seen it before. Right before you joined us, we had a guy empty his entire gun over there by the entrance." Abrams gestured to the door. "Wounded three officers. No one saw it coming. It came out later he was having some trouble at home with the wife wanting a divorce.

Apparently, he was mad about it."

"Is that why you hired me? To take his spot?"

Abrams pointed his index finger in the air. "As a matter of fact, yes. You're a little calmer. Although, you did punch me in the face outside of a bar, so who knows?"

"True, but I still can't believe Rick has gone mad. I guess your money theory is possible. I'm thinking about going out there to the mansion with Lily to check it out."

Abrams cocked his head. "Sounds like you don't have a choice. Did you ever find out who slashed her tires? Could there be a connection?"

"Lily thinks so. I was not able to get any leads on that event. She thinks Rick did it as a warning to her to stay off his case."

Abrams tapped the arm of the chair. "Not a bad theory. Who else would do that and why? Was anything stolen from the car? What would a random person's motive be to slash someone's tires?"

James sighed. "I know how it looks but I don't have evidence in either direction."

"And you don't really want to believe it."

"Correct."

"Good luck with that. And I would think with surveillance you have going on outside the funeral home there must be more than one person in on it—someone whose job is to transport bodies. Wouldn't you agree?"

"Yes, or they have their own accomplice helping them out with transport."

Abrams cocked his head to one side. "Wouldn't someone notice that? Seems to me like you have more people involved than you may have previously thought."

"If I go down there accusing more of her staff or

family, Lily might have my head on a stick. I'm going to let that one pan out."

"Sounds like it's getting a bit hairy. Let me know if you need any help interviewing people. I'm more impartial than you."

"Are you though?"

"Well, I can certainly act more impartial. And what if Rick is your bad guy? Who's going to house sit for you while you're on your honeymoon?"

"You." James pointed at Abrams. "Speaking of which, congratulations on your engagement. I thought this would never happen."

Abrams returned a sheepish grin. "Thanks. I still don't believe it either."

"There's still time to back out."

Abrams chuckled. "Sounds like something I'd say."

"Ugh." James slapped the table. "You know what that means? You're rubbing off on me."

"Consider it an honor. Do you need help searching the mansion?"

"No, we'll waste our own time. Plus you have a wedding to plan."

Abrams shook his head. "I don't know the first thing about that."

"I think as long as you show up, you're good."

"Even that is questionable."

"Nah, I don't buy it." James pointed a finger at Abrams's face. "There's a twinkle in your eye."

Abrams stood to leave. "That twinkle is from pure horror at how much company time you're wasting on this ritual theory."

"I still get everything else done on time and you said it yourself she's got good instincts."

"It's possible I was wrong."

James's eyes went wide. "No. *You*?"

"I said it was possible but very unlikely." He turned to leave. "Let me know if you find your snatcher among the weeds. I like ghost stories."

James chuckled. "Until you find out it's all true."

Abrams stopped in front of the door, then turned. "Then you better catch him."

****

James drove past a row of large homes on Sunshine Lane, each one grander than the previous. But none could compare to the Rubin mansion. Situated atop a hill, the sprawling gothic stone manor commanded attention despite its desolate existence. Now in different states of ruin, James wondered if anyone would bother saving it from crumbling away entirely.

He parked his car next to Lily's coupe. No doubt she wanted to get a head start without him. But her insistence on implicating Rick still weighed heavy on his mind and was creating quite the conflict within their marriage. He walked around the dried-up mermaid fountain in front of the house and made his way toward the back. He figured any sort of bad behavior would probably be going on in the rear of the house, not the front.

Once he turned the corner, the house had a different feel. The woods had stretched and overgrown into the backyard. An abundance of trees and plants blocked out the sun, making the air cool and damp. A disturbing breeze went down his shirt, making his back tremble. This did not feel like Sunshine Lane.

Lily stood, hands on her hips, a flame of hair blowing in wisps behind her. "About time."

A familiar twinge assaulted his belly. He felt a smile

creep onto his face. *Every time. She got him every time.*

He walked up to her, planting a peck on her lips. "Have you found anything?"

"Not yet but that's why I invited you to do the dirty work."

"This place gives me the creeps." He said, looking around at the overgrown grounds.

"I heard there's an underground wine cellar. Maybe I can go fetch you a bottle to ease your nerves."

"That won't be necessary, Mrs. Rivers. No one in his or her right mind should go inside that place. But this," he pointed to the dilapidated garden area that led into the woods, "has enough going on to attract some attention."

"It looks like the garden of hell. I want a closer look."

Lily headed to the grounds where stone benches barely visible among the vines and weeds lined its perimeter as if to one day swallow it whole. She held her leather jacket closed in the blowing breeze as she knelt to look at something she spotted on the ground. "Look at this." Her hands brushed away the weeds.

James approached her. He crouched down lower, blowing away some of the black dust with his breath. "Soot?"

"Looks like it. And it seems to stretch down that way." She pointed to her left as she exposed more of it from under the foliage. "There's a line of soot about four feet long."

"Maybe there was a long rectangular fire pit here that the Rubin's used from time to time for s'mores."

Lily gave him the side-eye. "Or maybe it's the remains of someone resembling Ms. Bernardo who happened to have been four feet tall."

"So you think it all went down here?"

"I think it's very likely. It's secluded, quiet, and has lots of space." Lily went back to analyzing the soot. "This happened recently. The weather hadn't had a chance to disturb the soot."

"I guess that makes sense. I would imagine one would need to dispose of the body rather quickly." James walked a few feet closer to where the garden ended and the wooded area began. The lines between them had blurred by the overgrown branches and the numerous brown crunchy leaves that had fallen to the ground and never cleaned up. A fair amount of garbage had also collected among the weeds and vines. Plastic bottles, used food containers, and random articles of clothing. None of it seemed to add up to any pattern in particular— although they could take some of it in for testing—until he noticed a fragment of paper with writing on it entwined within branches. Freeing it from nature's clutches, he turned it over in his hand. Barely discernible, he read the words out loud. "—join us on 10/5."

"What?" Lily asked, walking over to him. She snatched the paper fragment from his hand.

"Hey!" James complained.

"I don't believe it." She placed the fragment in her palm.

"What?"

"Don't you see? It's the brochure."

He frowned. "Oh, come on. You're seeing things your mind wants you to see."

"Look closer." She brought the top edge to his face. "That faded ink says Zeus."

James stared at the fragment. He could concede

there might be something there, but he couldn't tell what it said. "We'll take it in for analysis. But that's a stretch don't you think?"

She glared at him.

"What? I call it like I see it. I'm not totally convinced. And what does 10/5 mean?"

"It could be code for something? Or a date? It could be their next meeting date." She jumped up with excitement.

James shrugged. "Maybe. That's in two days."

"We have evidence that someone brought the brochure to the Rubin mansion." Her arms went out. "What more do you need?"

"Maybe George Rubin and his wife were members of this thing but that still doesn't prove anything bad happened here or that Rick had anything to do with it."

Her eyes lit up like silver daggers. *Scary.*

"I know how it looks. I agree with you but we're going to need more."

She walked back over to the line of soot, leaning over while walking up and down—which looked very uncomfortable.

"What's this?" She pointed to an area he hadn't yet explored. Standing up straight, she put her hand over her mouth. Her eyes went wide.

"Now what?" He made his way over to her. Had he been too skeptical? Had she found the true missing link?

"I think I know exactly what those are," she said, pointing to the ground.

He bent at the waist to get a closer look at the area she'd identified and then stood back up. He knew this was big, *very* big. *Huge.*

"Is that what I think it is?" she asked.

He didn't want to get her hopes up. "Possibly. We need to get them analyzed to know for sure."

"Bone fragments." The response came out on a bare whisper.

He nodded in agreement. "I'll make the call. We'll get this scene and the bones analyzed."

A smug look replaced the shock on her face.

"Really?" He couldn't believe her ego had swooped in so fast—or then again, yes, he could.

"Told you so."

The slight smile on her beautiful face was both infuriating and beautiful. He struggled to argue with her. "Must you do that?"

"Always and forever," she replied, petting the back of his head.

He sighed but couldn't keep his smile away. "I'm so lucky."

"And don't you forget it."

Chapter Nineteen

"What will you do?" Marcia's voice came out with a trembling shake.

Rick paced the floor of her apartment. "You have so little faith in me. How can this relationship keep growing or ever stand a chance if you don't believe in me?"

"I have faith in you but with cops all over the Rubin house there's no way we can go back there."

"Yes, I know. You don't think I know that?" Rick stopped pacing, cleared his throat and took a breath. He needed to calm down. If he lost Marcia, he'd never be able to pull off his plan. He noticed her eyes had become teary. "Don't worry. I'll figure everything out. This isn't the first time I've had to reinvent myself for The Cause."

In fact, before his detective days he'd been a smuggler, a burglar and an extortionist. He never got caught and he wasn't about to start now.

She looked up at him with puppy dog eyes. "It might be easier to let them win this time. We could get out now before things get out of hand. We could still be together."

Anger pulsed through his body.

Get out now? She needs to get out.

He hadn't failed at much but clearly inviting Marcia into his world had been a mistake. She might spoil everything if he didn't reel her in. Maybe a different approach was in order. "Now is not the time to underestimate me." He smiled. "Do you know what my last name means?"

She frowned. "Drakon? No, what does it mean?"

"It's Greek for dragon. That's how I like to think of myself, as a powerful being capable of smashing through any challenge. And that's why you should trust me. I will take us to where we want to be. If that means we change our ceremony's location, so be it. We'll adapt to any situation. But you have to trust me."

"I trust you but what if we lie low for a bit instead? Temporarily, while the cops are interested in us."

He turned away from her. Who did she think she was? He was the boss. He called the shots. "I can't do that. We've already done so much in preparation for the next ritual."

And I want the money.

Knowing he needed to regain control of the situation, he faced her. "Let's calm down for a minute. I want to let you in on a little secret."

"What kind of secret?"

"I've known James Rivers for years. I've been around him long enough to know some of his darkest moments."

Her expression remained blank.

"I know things he wants to keep buried. If James wants to keep things quiet in his perfect home, he and his wife will need to turn a blind eye to our activities."

Marcia frowned. "What do you know about him?"

"Don't worry about the details but if I know James, he falls hard for the ladies. He's not going to let anything come in between him and Lily, even if it costs him the case."

"Really? It's that bad?"

"Wouldn't you be upset if I hadn't been telling you

the whole truth about me?"

Her eyes darted back and forth. "I'm starting to think maybe I don't know enough. What have you been hiding?"

He knew this would come up eventually. "I'm not hiding anything. I'm an open book. What do you want to know?"

"Well…for starters I want to know how and why you got into rituals."

He took a seat on the couch across from her. If he wanted her in his life, for now he'd have to give her something in return. But he would give her the milder version—which wouldn't be easy. The con artist in him needed to take center stage.

He cleared his throat. "After my mom passed away, my dad decided to run an underground club for misfits looking for a place to bond with each other and network. I soon found that I loved hanging around troublemakers and outsiders. One of them, his name was Lucky, taught me how to clean and load a gun—a valuable skill within that crowd. My dad would charge admission, enough to make us some money to keep us afloat. From him I learned that people need and want to belong to something."

"If you liked living on the outskirts what made you want to be a detective? It seems that would be the opposite choice."

"True. As I got older life in the margins became less appealing. I wanted to go straight. I'd been on the other side of the law for so long it was time for a change."

Lies. He always loved power and money. The criminal life he grew up in never left him and becoming a detective had kept his enemies close.

"So now, by having these sacrificial rituals, you are providing a service for people that they want?" she asked.

"Exactly, I provide an outlet where people can gather and pray. The sacrifices cleanse the spirit, appease the gods and the followers believe this will positively impact their lives—to have the power of Zeus and the others look favorably upon them."

She took a deep breath. "I think it's a beautiful thing to give people what they expect to see, and I also want the gods to look favorably upon me but I'm going to be honest I haven't been feeling great about stealing bodies from the funeral home."

She can't start feeling guilty now, not right before our biggest turnout yet.

He got up to give her his signature shoulder rub. It usually helped to calm her down. "You can't worry so much. Remember, I got you into this and I'll get you out before anyone can do anything to you."

Her shoulders tensed beneath his fingertips. "What does that mean?"

"Nothing. I mean I've got a plan and we should be fine."

She looked up at him with a furrowed brow. "*Should be fine?* I need more than that." She stood and walked away from him. "I've taken a risk to be with you and support The Cause, but I also trusted you with my life."

"Relax, honey. Remember that everything you are doing is for The Cause, and that's the most important thing. We can't control everything, but our mission is to be pleased with our efforts no matter the cost."

Her arms went out in a pleading gesture. "I don't know if that's good enough. It feels like my whole life is flashing before my eyes."

Approaching her, he grabbed her hands. Although he wasn't the most affectionate person, he knew when to pull out the stops. His fingers intertwined with hers. "Stop. You need to trust me. If we don't have trust, we don't have anything."

"Tell me you'll cancel the next event," she pleaded. "You promised we could open our own funeral home one day. Let's run away from Manorview. We can go anywhere."

He took the gamble, confident his hold on her far exceeded her concerns. "Marcia, I'm not running away from anything. That's not me. I know what I promised and if we keep working for The Cause we can make enough money to do whatever you want. But if you want to end this, tell me to leave now."

She stared at the floor, seemingly contemplating her options. "I don't want you to leave. I want everything to be normal for us."

"It's never going to be normal for us. You'll have to accept that if you're ever going to be happy with me."

She looked at him. The desperation had left her eyes, replaced by reservation.

He'd laid it all on the table for her. But since she wasn't the type to stand on her own, he would rely on that for her continued loyalty. "I promise," he said, giving her hands a tight squeeze, "I'll do everything I can to make this plan work."

She gave him a slight smile but not much else.

He sighed with relief. Had he done enough to keep her in line? He thought so. "Deal?"

She nodded but stared at the floor, avoiding eye contact. "Deal."

"Good. I'll let you in on a little secret."

She raised her eyes to meet his.

"I've been looking around at funeral homes for sale outside of Manorview a little farther north."

She smiled wide. "Really?"

Lies.

"I've seen good options out there. But you just have to hold on a little longer."

She nodded. Her eyes twinkled. "In that case I will."

"That's my girl." He took her into a tight embrace. She needed to give him enough time to take the money and run. He believed she would.

Chapter Twenty

Normally, a trip to Gina's Beauty Bazaar meant stocking up on supplies for the funeral home. This time, Lily had other plans. Earlier this morning, while lying in bed, staring up at the ceiling and wondering who could help her case, it finally hit her—Gina Giordani. As an ex-gang member who used to live in New York City, Gina had to know something.

But will she talk?

As she entered the beauty supply shop, Lily had no idea if her scheme would work but if her friend could help in any way to shine the light on Rick, she would certainly try.

Gina looked up from her phone as Lily approached the counter. Strands of purple hair stood out against platinum blonde, and she wore oversized, black-framed glasses that made her look like a ladybug. With Gina, the look was never dull.

"How's it going?" Lily asked.

"Not bad. It's nice of you to stop in today. I finally got those bronzers you've been asking for."

"Oh, good. I've been wanting to give some of my clients a little sunshine on their cheeks." Lily glanced at her surroundings. She'd purposely come just after the store opened to avoid an audience.

Gina stared at her through black kohl-rimmed blue eyes. "What's wrong?"

"I need to speak with you…in private."

Gina stared for a second longer. She seemed to be grasping the gravity of the situation. "I'll close the store so we can chat in peace. My sales associate is off today." Making her way to the front door she locked the deadbolt and turned over the OPEN sign. "How can I help?"

"In the past you told me I could come by if I needed help. So here I am."

Gina's expression revealed nothing. She'd spent most of her life hiding in the shadows. Getting answers from her might be a challenge.

Her friend's eyes narrowed. "Is someone after you?"

"Not exactly. We have a…houseguest whom I believe is up to no good."

"Did he leave the toilet seat up?"

"I wish. He's been stealing bodies out of my funeral home and burning them in ritualistic sacrifices."

Gina's eyebrows shot up. "Geez. Nice houseguest. Where'd you find him?"

"I didn't. He's a friend of James."

"A friend?" Gina leaned toward Lily. "Maybe you should be looking even closer for your enemies."

"It might look that way, but James is in a bit of denial. He probably doesn't want to admit he's wrong either."

"Men never do. So how can I help?"

"I'm absolutely convinced Rick is the culprit based on suspicious behavior between him and some of my other employees and evidence I found in his room, but I need to know more about him. I want to catch him in the act. Would you know anything about him?"

Gina dragged in a breath. "What's his name?"

"Rick Drakon."

"Drakon? Is that Greek?"

Lily paused as her brain caught onto something. She'd recently come across some things written in Greek. Then it hit her. The flyer James showed her said Zeus at the top.

It couldn't be a coincidence.

She put that nugget of information away for the moment. "I'm not entirely sure but it sounds Greek. Have you heard of him? Oh, and I forgot to mention. He's also a detective."

Gina's jaw jutted out. "You've got a crooked cop? That makes things more difficult. No one is going to believe you."

"I realize that, but I know I'm right about him. The man is a criminal."

Gina put her index finger in the air. "On the other hand I know some people who might like to see a crooked cop go down. Let me make a phone call but first give me his description."

Lily blinked. "Uh, he's big, burly and bald."

Gina chuckled. "The three Bs?"

"And he wears a bold gold chain around his neck."

"I'll be sure to include that." She walked toward the back office. "Back in a second."

After the office door closed, Lily exhaled. She was glad she decided to get help—not an easy thing for her. A flurry of nervous energy flooded her body. Gina hadn't given away much but hopefully she'd discovered something.

Lily meandered over to the front door. She peered out the window. A line of customers had already formed outside. These people wanted their beauty products bad. She didn't blame them. Running out of your favorite mascara definitely could ruin your day.

A few more minutes went by before the office door opened.

"He's on the run," Gina announced triumphantly. "He's on the NYPD's list for crimes involving selling organs and other scams. This guy's trying to make money any way he can but he's not very good at it."

Lily's eyes opened wide. "I knew it." She blew all the air out of her lungs. "I knew I wasn't crazy. He's a wanted man living under my roof. Will they be coming after him?"

Gina cocked her head. "I never reveal anything—unwritten code, but I can't promise he won't be found. Your problem might resolve all on its own."

"Maybe, but that might take too long. He's stealing from my business. I need to know what his next move will be."

"You said he's been performing rituals?"

"That's probably how he's raking in the money—entrance fees. We think he was holding the rituals at the old Rubin mansion but now that the cops are all over it, looking for evidence of rituals, he's got to go somewhere else. You think he'll skip town again?"

"He might. On the call they said his place was raided and they found lots of pictures of cemeteries but when they went to check them out, they didn't find anything."

"Cemeteries?"

"The thought was maybe he was keeping money buried there or maybe bodies, but they never found anything."

"So he kept pictures of the cemeteries?"

Gina shrugged. "Who knows? Could be a weirdo or he's really good at getting rid of the evidence. I would consider checking out Manorview Cemetery. With lots of space, a creepy backdrop and no one else around, it seems like a great place to stage a ritual."

Lily nodded. "He's getting ready for another. And it'll be soon."

"Are you going alone? I wouldn't recommend it."

"You're probably right but it's complicated."

"At least take a gun."

Lily twisted her fingers.

Gina eyed her with suspicion. "You do know how to shoot a gun, right?"

Lily chuckled. "Of course."

"Well good. Take James's gun. If you need a refresher, you know where to find me."

Lily let out the air she'd been holding. "I might take you up on that offer. Listen, thanks. I won't take up anymore of your time."

Gina walked with her toward the entrance. "I meant what I said. Be careful. You might let the toughies sort it out instead of getting involved. It's no place for a small-town girl."

"You're probably right but I can't sit around waiting for him to steal my next client."

Gina opened the door and flipped the sign to OPEN. "Well, I warned you."

Lily looked at the eager customers ready to storm in and sighed. In some ways she wished her day could be as simple as getting instant gratification from purchasing a cosmetic product but no, she had to jump right into the most dangerous place she possibly could. She looked at Gina and smiled. "Thanks again. I'll see you soon."

Gina returned a knowing smile. "You know where to find me."

Chapter Twenty-One

Leaning against the doorframe leading into their bedroom, James asked, "When were you going to tell me you took my gun?"

Lily's cheeks flushed. She hated getting caught. "I thought you wouldn't notice for one night." She shrugged. "It's not like Manorview is teeming with criminals."

"Are you going to tell me *why* you took it?" James hadn't budged from the doorway, but he put his hands on his hips.

"I wanted to have a little more protection than I usually do when I go out into the field. This way you don't have to come and save me if things get hairy."

His eyes went wide. "I thought you weren't going to put yourself in *hairy* situations."

"That's very unrealistic. I'm not knitting on the side, you know. Besides, don't you want me to be more protected?"

He stood firm, concern etched on his face. "You're not going to tell me where you're going?"

"I'm following a lead. It probably won't pan out but it's definitely worth visiting."

James blinked a few times. "What lead?"

"We didn't know where Ri—I mean our cult leader would be holding his next ritual on October 5th, but I received information that the guy has a thing for cemeteries so I'm going to show up at Manorview Cemetery and see for myself."

"Cemeteries? Well, that rules out Rick. He doesn't have a thing for cemeteries."

"Maybe you don't know him as well as you think."

James rolled his eyes. "You're going armed? And you think all will be well?"

Lily shrugged. "Hoping."

James stepped into the room and leaned against the vanity. "Do you even know how to fire a weapon?"

A glimpse of his teasing lips made her armor drop. "I haven't fired one *yet,* but it can't be that hard."

"I'm still upset that you took my gun without asking but if you'd like I can show you how it works." He put his hand out for her to hand it to him.

She hesitated but then decided he was right. She had never fired one before. Why had she assumed it would be like riding a bicycle? Taking it out of the nightstand, she handed it over.

"Do you know if it's even loaded?"

"Look, I'm not dumb. Of course it's loaded. Why bother having it?"

"All right, all right. Let's go out back. Your living, breathing clients are gone for the day, right?"

"Yes, they have left."

Lily's tone brightened as she followed him down the stairs and out the back door. She'd expected him to give her a hard time for taking the gun, and maybe it would take some time for him to forgive her, but she believed after catching Rick in the cemetery, James would have no choice but to forgive her. Luckily, she didn't even have to do all that.

The cool evening breeze whipped through her hair

as they stood in the parking lot of the funeral home. Even better, the backyard had a nice set of tall columnar evergreen trees blocking the neighbors' view of their lesson.

"We're not going to fire a round out here—talk about small town gossip. But we can unload it and practice so you can get comfortable. You're probably not going to fire more than a few rounds, if that, but this is how you take out the magazine." He pressed a small button on the side and the magazine slid out. He put it in his back pocket.

"There's a bullet in the chamber." He pulled the slide back exposing the bullet and let it drop out from the chamber onto the ground. "There, now it's unloaded." He let the slide return to firing position. "Since this is a semi-automatic, you won't need to reload the magazine for every shot. But to load it you would reverse the steps I just did. Now to shoot. Stand here," he pointed to a spot in front of him.

Lily did what she was told and waited for further instruction. His body pressed into her back while his breath warmed her ear.

Gun lessons aren't so bad.

He lifted his right arm out in front of her with the barrel pointing directly in front of them. "Take the pistol in your right hand."

She followed orders and gripped the handle.

"That's too low. Grip it higher for better control on recoil."

Lily had no idea what he was talking about, but she listened and moved her hand farther up the gun.

Keeping his right hand over hers, he then guided her left hand toward the weapon until he had completely encompassed her body. "Now, the left hand covers the fingers of your right hand to add even more stability."

She stopped breathing. James may be mentally struggling to give her this lesson, but his body sure didn't let on.

"Keep your elbows slightly bent and keep the trigger in the ready position."

"What does that mean?"

"It means the trigger has some slack. It will take longer to fire in between shots if you don't keep the trigger pulled taut. Try it."

Lily slid her index onto the trigger and slowly pulled until she felt resistance.

"Feel it?"

His voice was so close to her ear it gave her goosebumps. She struggled to contain the shiver in her arms and to keep them pointed on the target. By now, the warmth from his body had generated enough heat for the both of them in the crisp fall air. She could feel his muscles pressing into her back.

"I feel it."

"Keep both eyes open on the target and take a breath."

She breathed in his familiar soap and shaving cream scent—both made with mouth-watering spice and musk.

Focus!

He took one small impossible step toward her, setting her stomach on fire. "Shoot."

She pulled the trigger. The gun clicked. Her breath spilled out all at once. That's all it took to end a life—not a great feeling but she hoped it wouldn't come to that.

He spun her around to face him. Lips crushed hers in a burst of heated urgency. She dropped the firearm as her arms went around his neck. His hands weaved through her hair and then moved down pressing against her back. An eternity of frustration was wiped away in their embrace.

"Wait," Lily pulled away. "Does this mean you believe me?"

James blinked a few times. "Believe you?"

"About Rick."

James looked up at the darkening sky. Then he looked down at her with an intensity she hadn't seen in a while—the blue depths of which she could fall into forever. He nodded. "I believe you."

"You do?" A smile stretched across her face. "I knew you'd come around."

"Now hold on there. You haven't actually produced any real proof that will hold up in court."

"What?" She took a step back. "You just taught me how to use a gun." She pointed at the pistol lying in the grass. "Why would you do that if you didn't want me to do something about it?"

He got closer to her. "I wanted to be near you." His breath in her ear sent chills all over her body.

How can she be mad? The fight left her body before she could take another breath.

"I believe you," he continued, "but I still hold out hope that you are wrong."

"Don't you want to be a united front?"

"You know how I feel about accusing Rick."

"Even with my track record?"

"Good point. But you are human…most of the time."

She smiled. "More like superhuman and besides, I like proving you wrong."

"I know you do. Now that I think about it, forget everything I just taught you."

"Not a chance." Lily picked up the gun. "With so much at stake I think I might need *more* practice."

He gave her a smoldering glance. "What kind?"

"You'll have to follow me to find out. It's warmer inside though." She raised the weapon with the barrel pointed to the ground. "I'm bringing this."

As she turned to walk toward the back door of the house, he followed. "Of course you are."

Chapter Twenty-Two

Startled from a sound sleep, Lily's eyes snapped open. Dim light peeked through the window blinds, meaning it was early—way too early. Today was October 5th. The day she planned to bust Rick and his entire operation.

So as not to disturb her husband, she gently rolled over and looked into his peaceful, sleeping face. Would he go with her? Or would he pretend to let her have the glory—then follow her anyway? She hoped not. They were supposed to work together. With the honeymoon only days away she wondered if her actions tonight would ruin the whole thing.

His eyes popped open—a sea of blue against ink black hair. "Morning." His voice came out rough. His hand brushed her arm.

"Is it?"

"What is your plan anyway?" The rubbing stopped. "Are you going to show up with a gun that you barely know how to use and hope Rick is there burning bodies among a group of people in the cemetery? What if they all have guns and collectively point them at you. What then?"

Lily sighed. She knew he was right. She shouldn't go alone. She'd gotten caught up in his reluctance to implicate Rick, but if he really did believe in her, James should go with her.

She rolled her eyes, hating the next words out of her mouth. "Will you come to the cemetery tonight?"

James smiled. "I can't believe my ears."

"Just this once."

"It shouldn't be just this once. This is how it should always be, you and I working together. We talked about this remember? And don't worry, you'll get all the glory *if* your theory pans out."

"I don't want the glory, but I will gladly say I told you so."

He resumed rubbing her arm. "I wouldn't expect any less."

****

Later, as the sunlight dimmed and the air grew crisp, Lily stared down at the gun where it lay on her bedroom vanity. Would it help subdue the man she'd been obsessing over and finally end his reign of terror? She could only hope.

"Did you load it?" James asked.

"I figured it out."

"I'll take that as a yes." His smile widened. "I have a surprise for you." He placed a hard case on the vanity.

Lily eyed it with suspicion. "What is it?"

"It's not a diamond necklace but I think you'd prefer this in any event." James opened it. "You get one of your own. Same model, courtesy of Manorview PD."

Her eyes went wide as she observed the new gun. "How did you manage that?"

"Now that you're on the payroll, you get a gun. Consider yourself lucky. Most new recruits have to buy their own."

Lily came out of her chair with a shout. "Payroll?

I'm on the payroll?"

"Abrams finally came through. He had to go all the way to the top for approval. When he showed the chief how much work you contributed, including your help in solving a cold case, he had no choice but to approve it."

"I can't believe it." She jumped into his arms. "I actually sound credible now?"

James cocked his head. "Well, you're accusing a detective and a friend of—"

"All right. You've made your point already. I know you hate my theory, and you sort of believe me, but I'm still going to pursue it."

James smiled. "I know you will."

"But thank you for all of this."

"You're welcome. It's loaded so you're all set. When do we leave, Boss Lady?"

Lily grabbed her new gun. It was the same make and model as James's but hers had a glossy new shine to it. "We leave now."

****

The silent ride to the cemetery made James uneasy. He'd agreed to a plan that he had no intention of following. She said she wanted to go first, to see Rick with her own eyes, performing the ritual she'd obsessed over for the last few days. But the more time she spent on the field alone, the more she'd be exposed to danger. On the other hand, if she was wrong about Rick, letting her go first would minimize her disappointment. But in the end, her safety came first.

"I think coming here a little earlier was the right move," she said, checking her gun and replacing it in her new shoulder holster as they parked near the entrance of the cemetery. "That way the followers won't get in the way of Rick's arrest."

Even though he'd been integral in getting her the new weapon, he didn't have to like it. "You still want me to stay back?" He already knew the answer. The determination in her eyes said enough.

"I've got this. Don't worry. I've been thinking about this moment for days." She put her hand on the door handle but paused before leaving the vehicle and then turned back to look at him. "I'll be careful."

He could tell she needed some reassurance. "I'll be here if you need me."

She smiled and gave him a soft peck on the lips.

Although unexpected, he welcomed her moment of uncertainty. It meant she knew her limitations and more importantly, that she needed him.

Without another word she jumped out of the car, her posture exuding renewed confidence. He had to hand it to her—she was fearless.

After she left, the silent darkness enveloped him. A creepy vibe had invaded his confidence, making him want to reverse his car and drive back home. But he wouldn't leave her here with whatever monster might be lurking in the dark.

Secretly, he hoped Rick had nothing to do with this and instead they would either find some other lunatic— or nothing. Fearing his old friend might be involved made James question his own convictions. He rubbed at his face and bounced his knee with nervous energy. An audible sigh escaped his lips as his head fell back on the headrest.

Frustrated, he closed his eyes and pinched the area above his nose. He didn't want to take over or interrupt, but it should only take Lily a minute to assess the scene and report back. The agony of not knowing the outcome or if she was safe killed him.

Nope, he couldn't wait any longer. Taking his gun out of its holster, he stepped out of the car.

No matter how many times he'd infiltrated the bad guys, it never got any easier. His heart pounded into his throat every time. Up ahead a huge mausoleum stood at the bottom of a hill. He ran through the grass and tombstones keeping his body low and quiet. When he reached the back of the mausoleum he stopped to listen.

Crying? Is someone crying?

He held up his gun and squeezed it tighter as he prepared to run into the fray.

"It's all right. You can tell me. You're safe now."

He knew that voice anywhere—Lily. Relieved to hear she was not the one crying, he turned the corner to face the other person standing there.

"Marcia?" he asked, pointing his gun down at the ground.

Lily crossed her arms across her chest. Her gun was out of sight. "You can't stand down, can you?"

James shrugged. "I heard crying. What kind of person would not react to that?"

Marcia sniffled.

"She was about to tell me where Rick is hiding."

James took in the scene surrounding them. A cool breeze infiltrated the collar of his shirt. With it came a shiver, and the scent of rotting eggs and sulfur. Living above a funeral home made him an expert to the smell of a corpse badly in need of a burial. Peering around Marcia, he observed two long forms wrapped in white cloth and laying on a stone circle in front of the mausoleum. The two stolen bodies.

He turned his attention back to Marcia who continued weeping. He noticed she was clad all in black and had a ski mask rolled up onto the top of her head.

Just who is the ringleader?

"There's no mistaking what's about to go down here." He gestured toward the bodies. "Is Marcia Zeus?"

She said nothing as the tears continued to pour down her cheeks.

"I can't believe you're still trying to save Rick," Lily yelled. "There's no way she's in this alone."

"I'm calling it like I see it," he snapped back.

"Marcia, it's going to be very difficult to prove you weren't involved," Lily said. "James is right. This doesn't look good. If you take us to Rick, it will look better to the judge. Don't protect someone who doesn't care if you take the fall."

Marcia blinked a few times, keeping her eyes on Lily as if she were considering a switch in allegiance. From what James knew about Marcia's temperament, she could be easily swayed onto their side, but he'd let Lily take the lead on this one.

Marcia sucked in a breath, then blurted, "I told him this would happen. He didn't listen."

"That's what criminals do," Lily told her. "I tried to warn you. He has created so much trouble for you. Don't you see it?"

Marcia nodded as more tears dropped onto her cheeks. "I thought he loved me. Then I began to notice he loved his church, not me."

"Church? It's a cult and not a very good one. He's a scammer, not a preacher. All of this," Lily spread her arms out wide, "is false. There is no church. The sooner you accept that, the better for you."

James stepped closer to them. "Tell us now, Marcia. Where is he?"

She kept her eyes down. "I'll take you to him."

"James, why don't you stay here and call for backup. The followers will be showing up soon and someone needs to stay with the bodies."

"Stay here?"

"Yes, that way you won't feel awkward or hesitate around Rick."

James opened his arms out in protest. He didn't know if he should feel insulted or comforted. "Hesitate?"

She came to him, placed both palms on his chest, and stared up into his eyes. "Not too long ago you considered him a friend. I don't want all those feelings—although justified—to get in the way. He's a criminal and I'm going to get him." At that, she looked away. "Marcia, let's go."

James said nothing as he watched them leave; he knew better than to try and stop her. Luckily, he'd already planned on having Abrams on standby. As a newly engaged person, he trusted Abrams to know what was at stake. Everything.

After he called the crime scene investigators, James stood near the bodies to make sure nothing else happened to them. Seeing what Rick had planned for the evening made his skin crawl. To think there were people who actually wanted to stand here and watch a cremation? Those people clearly were under his spell. It wouldn't be the first time in history people mindlessly followed a fanatic ruler—but hearing about it was one thing.

Experiencing it was something else.

He had seen terrible things in his career; things that kept him up at night. But this was different. His friend had committed heinous crimes right under his nose while James remained oblivious—and made excuses for him.

He'd have to learn to live with himself.

After several minutes passed the appointed time and no one arrived on scene, he began to wonder if the cult even had any followers—or if they'd been tipped off. Until two young women turned the corner of the mausoleum. As soon as they saw him, they stopped in their tracks and looked like they might rabbit.

"Don't do it," he warned, gesturing with a raised palm. "Manorview PD. This is an investigation. Let's see some ID."

One had stringy blonde hair and wore jeans and a white T-shirt. The one on her right had short, wavy brown hair, green cargo pants and a blue long-sleeved shirt.

"I'm Laura and this is Jane," the stringy blonde said. "We were taking a walk and took a wrong turn. We'll just be on our way—"

"Wrong turn? Into a cemetery? I find that hard to believe."

They both looked at the ground.

"Your leader is about to be arrested. I suggest you both be straight with me."

Laura's eyes went wide as saucers. She'd given herself away fairly easily. "We were just curious. No harm in that. We heard about the Greek dude's shows and wanted to see for ourselves."

James craned his neck. "Greek dude's shows? You two aren't regulars?"

After sharing a glance, Jane said, "I've never met a follower, but we heard about it."

"You were curious?" James asked with the tone of a

skeptic. "What did you think was going to happen here?"

Laura shuffled her feet. "I heard this guy performs human sacrifices out here in the cemetery." Her arms went wide. "It sounded crazy, so we came out to see for ourselves."

Again, he wondered if someone had tipped them off. The number of followers couldn't be large. His guess was Rick. He would be the only one who cared enough to keep them around in case he was forced to take his rituals elsewhere.

"Neither of you knows anyone who claims to be a follower of this little ritual?"

"No." Laura shook her head. "A friend from work heard about it from her mom but neither of them actually believed it was real." Laura craned her neck at the mounds behind James. "It looks like it might be true."

James moved to block her view. "This scene is under investigation. We're collecting evidence and have not made any conclusions as of yet. I'd like to talk to your friend from work at some point."

Laura shrugged. "Sure. She doesn't know anything. It's all rumors."

"Where do you work?"

"The movie theater on Sycamore Street."

"Both of you work there?"

Jane nodded. "Yes, I do, too."

"All right, there's nothing to see here. Show me some ID, then go back about your business. I'll keep your information in case I have more questions."

After the two girls left, James realized he was dealing with someone far more capable than he'd once believed. He needed to meet the people who'd risk everything to support a sicko. But not today. In a town full of secrets the followers would melt back into society like nothing ever happened.

Without anyone credible to question James had nothing to go on.

Chapter Twenty-Three

"He's been staying with you?" Lily asked.

Marcia nodded as the elevator in her building rose to her floor. "Rick told me things were getting hostile at the funeral home, so I told him he could stay with me."

"Hostile? More like suspicious." Lily watched the elevator numbers light up one after another, then glanced at Marcia's tear-stained cheeks. "I get it. He promised you the world but what he gave you was hell. I don't know how you stayed with him this long, but we'll fix it. I'll fix it."

Lily knew Marcia would never be able to work for her again and she would need one hell of a plea bargain to avoid serious jail time. How did it come to this?

As the elevator stopped on the twelfth floor, Lily's pulse rate sped up. Rick hated her. She'd been the only one to pursue him. If it weren't for her, he'd still be hanging out in the funeral home, stealing bodies while she and James go on a honeymoon. Who knows, maybe he would've burned the whole place down. Her jaw clenched.

Good.

She needed to use any anger she could muster for this meeting. She turned to Marcia as they stood in front of her apartment door. Lily's hand slid the gun out of its holster. Lord knows she would need it. "You knock on the door and answer him when he asks who's there. That's the only way he will open it."

Marcia eyed the gun and then sighed as if her life was about to tumble down on her like a ton of bricks. Even though Lily hated what Marcia had done, she would lead them to Rick, and they would finally get rid of the boogeyman.

At first, Marcia gave two wimpy raps on the door.

"That's not going to do it. Louder."

She tightened her fist and pounded harder on the door. No answer. "It's me, Marcia," she announced at the door.

There was a pause and a few tentative footsteps coming closer and closer to the door until it finally swung open. Lily held her gun pointed at the man she'd been chasing. Rick Drakon.

He smiled at Lily. Then frowned at Marcia. "I knew you were weak. It took so little to get you to talk."

Saying nothing, Marcia stared at the ground.

"She did the right thing," Lily said.

He turned to Lily. "You have nothing. It's her word against mine. Didn't you see? She burned those bodies. Not me."

Keeping the gun pointed at Rick, Lily forced her way into the apartment. She thought about the black T-shirt she'd found in Shanna's old room. Had Marcia worn it instead of Rick?

"She may have done the dirty work, but you are without a doubt, the ringleader. It takes a true coward to prey on the weak."

Rick's posture relaxed. He seemed less concerned about the turn of events but the arrogant stance made her uneasy. She kept the gun pointed at him, although her hand shook with uncertainty. Could she kill a man if she had to? Not if she had a choice. "With Marcia's help, we have more than we need."

He smirked. "As I said before, it's my word against hers."

"Your DNA will be all over her apartment and with her confession your involvement will be easy to prove."

"In fact," he continued without missing a beat, "coming here with a gun pointed at me when I've not behaved in an aggressive manner is unprofessional."

"You are a flight risk and a manipulator. Not to mention you are clearly unwell if you think stealing bodies from my funeral home is normal behavior."

"Ah, so protective of your funeral home. So this," he said as his dark eyes flickered to the gun, "is personal. If that's what you care about, Lily, I can get *real* personal."

"What are you talking about?"

Rick gave her a self-assured grin. "You don't even know who you are sleeping with."

Her eyes narrowed. What bomb was Rick about to drop that would change her life forever? "Stop talking. This case is clearly closed."

He shrugged his shoulders. "Even better since according to you I have nothing to lose. I'm talking about James. He and I have known each other for years. And boy, does he have a past."

The pounding in her ears left her practically deaf. "Everyone does. Even you. Anyway, I know about his past. He told me everything. Nothing you can say will change anything."

"But he didn't tell you everything. And what he didn't tell you will break you two apart."

Lily's chest heaved. The hatred oozing from Rick's stare made her want to question everything she had known about James. But she couldn't let him get to her. "This is a sad attempt to take the heat off yourself."

Rick smiled. "I may have done some things in my day, but my past is not nearly as pathetic as your husband's."

The sound of racing footsteps approached the open doorway. Lily didn't dare take her eyes off Rick. Whoever it was would need to look away and move along.

"Pathetic is exactly what I would call you," her husband's voice rang out from behind her.

"Buddy, you don't believe these accusations against me, do you?" Rick asked with a far less creepy tone.

"At first, I didn't want to but then I thought about it," James said as he came closer. "You've been cryptic about what you've been up to here and partnering up with Marcia doesn't add up"

Rick laughed loud and long. "All you have here are assumptions. I came out here to help you with your honeymoon plans and this is how I get treated?" He spread his hands in a gesture of surrender. "What I know about you, James, will harm your marriage. It will be my get out of jail card."

Lily watched her husband's nostrils flare. "No deal. You can't hold anything over me. I think you came here to rip off some naïve innocents and satisfy some God-complex, not to do us a favor."

Rick's expression turned cold.

As he turned his eyes on Lily—a lump formed in her throat. Her stomach roiled. Whatever he had to say held more power than pointing a gun to his face.

"Did you know you married a liar?"

Lily swallowed hard but said nothing.

"Or maybe you want to tell her, James? How you married her without even telling her you're a junkie."

The shaking in her hands had become so unbearable, Lily felt forced to lower her gun. She'd already told herself no matter what James had kept from her, it wouldn't change anything.

James's voice seethed with anger. "You're sinking this low out of desperation."

"Maybe, but it's still the truth."

"I'm not a junkie. Yes, I went through some things after Andrea's death, like any normal person would. I certainly didn't hurt anyone, only myself. You, on the other hand, are a parasite, preying on the weak for your own gain."

Lily glanced at James. She wasn't angry. Her heart felt heavy for him.

"Once a junkie, always a junkie," Rick taunted. "If Lily had known, would she have married a junkie? If I leave you with that doubt forever instilled in your brain, rotting and festering, then it was all worth it."

Lily saw James's jaw clench in time to his pumping fists. *Oh boy.*

The elevator dinged as the door opened on Marica's floor. Teeth gritted, James lunged forward but stopped just short in front of Rick who stood his ground. Abrams gripped James's arms with power Lily had never seen him display.

"Now, now. Don't batter the suspect. Even if he is a freak." Abrams said, with the calm voice of a veteran.

"Again, you can't connect me to your scene," Rick said. "All you have is Marcia. It's her word against mine.

She became a scorned woman after I dumped her. Nothing more."

Marcia stepped in; tears welled in her eyes. "Not true. You were groomed to be a thief and a scam artist. That's what you have become. You are not Zeus or anything powerful. I'm sorry I ever met you."

Lily watched the former weak woman assert herself in a nice change of pace. She'd come a long way from the wide-eyed deer caught in headlights to sticking up for her beliefs. She made a lot of mistakes that will cost her dearly but at least there seemed to be a glimmer of hope that she could come out of this a stronger, better person.

"Take him away," Abrams said to the backup team waiting in the hallway. "We have more than enough to charge him."

Rick smiled. "You've got nothing. Your criminal is there." He pointed at Marcia. "She did everything." Two large officers pushed their way in and handcuffed Rick. "You'll see. This is a mistake." He scowled at Marcia but went without a fight.

Lily breathed out a sigh of relief. She hadn't known how Rick would react. The thought that she might have to shoot him had crossed her mind. Her hand shook as she held the gun. And yet there was so much she still had to process. She couldn't look at James, not yet.

"We'll have to take you in, too," she told Marcia. "You'll get a deal for your cooperation in this case, but you may have to do some time."

The idea that Marcia may have been the one lighting the match to her clients' bodies seemed impossible and revolting at the same time.

Marcia looked down at the floor. "I know. I'm sorry

for everything. Once I realized Rick didn't really care about our future, I saw nothing but the end of us. I should've listened to you, but I thought I loved him. And now I'll have to live with the horrible things I've done."

"I know you thought you loved him and yes, you did despicable things. He took so much from you. I hope one day when you start over you will be a better judge of people's character and make better decisions."

Lily glanced toward James. He'd been staring at her with increasing intensity. Suddenly she was uncomfortable in her own skin.

Marcia nodded and covered her eyes with her hands.

"On that note," Abrams clapped his hands together. "I think I'll head back to the cemetery and begin arranging the return of your two missing clients." He pointed at Lily.

"Good idea," James said, breaking his silence.

"Sounds like a big job," Lily said looking at James. "Why don't you go with him? I'll take Marcia to the station."

James didn't answer.

"Good," Abrams said. "I always need some help in my old age."

But judging by his hold on James earlier Lily knew that wasn't true. Although she didn't think Abrams knew about James's substance abuse, she could tell he knew something was up.

"Sure thing." James walked slowly toward the door. "It also gives me a chance to admit to myself that I was wrong about Rick and Lily was right…again."

"No one is shocked about that." Abrams slapped James on the back and pushed him through the door. "Get used to it."

Chapter Twenty-Four

Lily stared at the sparkling clear water from the bungalow. The water line on the horizon went into infinity. She and James left for Hawaii soon after Rick's apprehension. The flight had been quiet. It seemed her husband wanted to give her time to process the new information—and she'd been more than glad to do so.

The shock had already passed. She felt more pain for him than herself. Anger didn't seem to fit either since she did not feel betrayed. Lost would be a better word. Had she really known James? Had she known enough to marry him? Those questions bounced around in her head as James came out to the deck to join her on a recliner chair.

"Beautiful here. I could stare at this view all day," he said, rolling up the sleeves of his white linen shirt.

She'd never seen him looking so casual and inviting. She could stare at *him* all day. "It is beautiful. I'm glad we came."

"I wanted our honeymoon to be special. You work hard and we both deserved some time away. I hadn't expected Rick would turn into the boogeyman. Obviously, I wouldn't have invited him into our world had I known all the trouble he had in store."

"You had no suspicions he'd been heading up a fake church? Was it something his family passed on to him?"

James shrugged. "I had no suspicions. I found out about his family's unrelated crimes, but he largely went under the radar. He fooled everyone enough to become a detective. Who knows? Maybe deep down he wanted to change for the better but couldn't keep the demons away. He had me fooled. It makes me question the instincts I thought I had." He stared down at his bare feet. "It makes me question everything."

"You have good instincts, but you were blinded by the friendship you thought you had with him. I could be more objective in this case, which is why I wanted to take the lead."

He gave her a side-glance. "You'd want the lead regardless, but I don't disagree. Once again, the Reynolds Funeral Home lives to fight another day."

"We lost a few clients in that fight though. Those families have to live with the horror of knowing their loved ones were used in some weird financial ploy. From that the business will suffer some fallout."

"You'll recover and you did save two of the four bodies that went missing," he said, raising the first two digits on his right hand. "That should count for something."

"And we lost Marcia in the fray. That means more of the makeup work will fall on me."

"So we'll hire someone else, someone who is a little more sure of themselves. How about Gina? She owns a beauty store and seems to know her way around makeup. She seems like a good fit."

Lily nodded. "She would be a good fit. Not a bad idea. If I can pry her away from her beauty shop and convince her to apply makeup on the dead."

"Maybe even on a part-time basis. It's worth a try.

You never know." He held his hands up in surrender. "See, I'm not totally useless."

Lily's smile vanished. She could tell he was prolonging *the* conversation they needed to have with small talk. She glanced at the sunlit sea, garnering as much tranquility as she could from its beauty, before facing him. "Were you ever planning on telling me?"

There. She said it.

He sucked in a breath and gave her a long stare. She could see the pain in his eyes.

"I knew I would, but I didn't know how or when. I put it off in hopes of burying it for as long as I could. It's not something I am proud of."

"For how long did you self-medicate, James?"

He looked at his feet again. "A year. Right after Andrea died, while I still lived in New York City. I'm sure people at work knew but they looked the other way. I confided in Rick but of course I had no idea his demons were far worse than mine. He'd kept my secret and then used it to try and bail himself out of trouble."

"How did you stop?"

His knee bounced like a jackrabbit running from a predator. "I got sick of myself. One day I'd had enough and never looked back. October 28th—the first day I went clean."

"That date is coming up. We need to celebrate."

He nodded. "It is and I'm proud of that."

"And you never went back or had a bad day since?"

"No, I'm not even tempted. As I had told you when we met, I don't really drink much. Maybe an occasional beer here and there but that's it. I don't have it in me to go back there."

Lily stared back out to sea. An orange glow bathed

her skin as the sun began to set. She hoped with every fiber of her being that he would never need to go back to that dark place. She'd have to trust him.

"Rick was right," he said.

She turned back to him. "About what?"

"He knew I was afraid to tell you and he was right. Granted, it's not something I'm worried about falling into again, but I should've told you. For that I'm sorry."

"Especially since you had sworn off dating civilians after what happened with Andrea. But look at you now. Married and on your honeymoon."

"I'm so fortunate. Things could have gone a different way for me. You came into my life and changed the trajectory in so many ways. I thought I'd be lost forever." He leaned forward, brushing her knees with his fingers. "And that's why you never have to worry because I know what I have to lose."

Her heart swelled to the point where there was no room for doubt.

"So are we good, detective?" he asked.

"Oh, that reminds me. I've decided I don't want to be on the payroll at Manorview PD."

He leaned back in his chair. "I thought that's all you ever wanted."

"I thought so, too, but I decided I kind of like being clandestine."

"You're not really clandestine. I thought you wanted to appear more legitimate to the victims."

"I did but I kind of like having one foot in the door. I think my talents lie in discovery, the rest I can leave up to you. Plus, I'm no good with a gun." She thought back to the few times her heart landed in her throat when she had to act like she had control of the scene and *boy,* had that been a farce. "I can't seem to get used to the idea of killing someone. I think I'll leave that part to you."

"Oh, thanks. I'll be the murderer." He smiled. "But actually, I guess that makes me feel a little better. It means you need me."

"I always need you. Unless there is anything else you're hiding?"

"Not a thing. You know me inside and out."

Lily smiled. "Same." She lay back in her seat, letting the setting sun's rays envelope her. Her mind at peace, she decided she could put their issues to rest. Everyone had a past. How they chose to deal with it was what mattered, and James had dealt with his. At least for now.

"You wanna go sunset swimming?"

The idea of him peeling off his shirt made her jump right out of her chair. "Now you're talking. Let's go."

He grabbed her hand as they made their way to the edge of the dock. The wooden planks exposed to the sun all day burned her feet as she hopped toward the water, but she didn't care. Nothing could ruin their honeymoon in her eyes, not even the darkest demons of the past. She watched him peel off his shirt and make his way to the edge of the dock. They'd spent most of their honeymoon in their bathing suits and today was no exception.

"Whoops," she said as her hands pushed on his back.

"Hey!" He fell toward the water but had managed to grab her hand and take her down with him.

The cool water stung as she plowed through the surface but as she kicked and pushed her way up her skin had already adjusted, and the water relaxed her muscles.

When he resurfaced his wide grin said it all. "If I go down, you're going down with me. We're a team, remember?"

She wiped away the water from her eyes. She should have known he would rise to her challenge. Any slight annoyance she'd felt when he pulled her into the water quickly faded away as she wrapped her legs around his waist and hooked her arms around his neck. His eyes matched the cerulean sea, knocking her guard down to nothing. "How could I forget?"

****

One week later, Lily found herself staring at the black T-shirt she'd seen in Shanna's bedroom during her snoop fest—the one with the burnt stench. After the room had been searched it had been brought into the station where it was logged in as evidence.

"What the matter?" James asked from his desk.

Lily let out a breath. "It's way too big."

He put down his pen. "What is?"

"The sooty T-shirt."

"The one that smells like burnt bodies?"

Lily nodded. "Marcia is five foot three at the most. This shirt wouldn't fit. It's huge."

"Are you saying she couldn't have worn it?"

"She could've but it would've been awkward. Why would she choose to wear a shirt that didn't fit her?"

"Maybe she borrowed it."

"From whom? Rick?"

"Maybe."

Lily cocked her head as she stared at James, still defending Rick.

James rolled his eyes. "So Rick wore it all along?"

"Rick or someone else. But probably him, yeah."

James came over to take a look for himself. "It's quite large. But she could've borrowed it from him."

"Maybe. Or she's hiding something."

James sighed. "Never a dull moment."

"It can't hurt to talk to her. I have a funny feeling there's more to the story."

"Naturally. Well, you know where to find her. Cell two. Do me a favor, don't go feeling bad for her and let her out. I know you've decided to back off a bit on the sleuthing but letting a prisoner escape won't go over well around here."

She slapped his shoulder. "I'm not going to let her out. I want to know what actually happened." She shrugged her shoulders. "Maybe there are others involved?"

"I know. You're right." He sighed. "But can we go back to Hawaii now?"

"Yes, please. As soon as I wrap this up," Lily said and made her way to cell two.

Rick had been transferred to a larger prison facility farther upstate for extra security. Facing him here may have been too difficult—although when she thought about what her clients had gone through, she may have liked to have a few words alone with him. She had fewer reservations about Marcia's criminal prowess, but it still made her knees quake to approach the bad guy or girl in their jail cell. And every time she walked down these halls she wondered if her dad had had the same fears when he walked down the same corridor before he was brutally murdered. Her guess was no. A stoically brave cop, he never appeared afraid to her—at least that was what she remembered. He was a real cop. She was not.

Lily stopped at cell two. Marcia's tiny frame appeared out of place inside a jail cell. But she had been quite the wild card and her life hadn't turned out the way Lily had expected. She had underestimated her and miscalculated, a mistake she would not repeat in the future.

"Marcia, can I have a word with you?" She watched the woman's small body stir from a seated position. She didn't reply. "I'm glad you are cooperating with us. It's the right thing to do but I have some questions about some of the logistics of the rituals."

Marcia stayed quiet.

"First of all, how were you and Rick able to transport the bodies out of my funeral home without anyone knowing?"

"Rick paid Antonio to transport the bodies in the hearse so that no one would suspect anything."

Lily's heart sank. "Antonio Reales? How did Rick manage that? Antonio was very loyal to us."

Marcia shrugged. "I liked him a lot. He talked about wanting to buy a house for his mom. I guess everyone has a price."

"Unfortunately, he made things more difficult for himself. I wish he had come to me and asked for a raise."

"I doubt that would've been enough." Marcia mumbled.

"Maybe not." Lily sighed. She figured someone had to be helping them. For a brief moment she'd feared it had been her little brother but finding out it had been Antonio didn't make her feel that much better. She switched gears. "Are you aware that my tires were slashed the night I discovered you with Rick at Marco's restaurant?"

Marcia nodded slowly.

"We didn't have enough evidence to prove who did it. But it's no shock that the same night I find you two together on a date my tires get slashed. Was it Rick?"

She nodded again. "It happened so fast. He seemed like a rabid animal. There was no way I could even argue about it with him. He just lost it."

Hearing how Rick had been so irked by her presence sounded delightful despite how expensive it had been to replace those tires—probably still worth it. "That should've been your first clue about him."

Marcia blinked hard. She seemed tired and annoyed of being lectured. "He apologized for his behavior and said it would never happen again."

Lily decided to move on. "We recovered a black T-shirt from Shanna's bedroom where Rick had been staying. The shirt was of particular interest because it carried a very distinct burn smell. I thought for sure it was worn during a ritual. The question is, who was wearing it? I know you said that you were the one performing the rituals under Rick's instruction, but the T-shirt is clearly not your size. If you were given the task by Rick, why would you choose to wear something four times your size? Doesn't seem like a choice one would voluntarily make."

Marcia hesitated, and then she took in a breath. "That's because he wore it, not me."

Lily gripped the bars. She couldn't believe what she was hearing. "Rick wore the shirt? As in, he was at the rituals, not you?"

Marcia nodded. Her upper lip quivered. "He performed the rituals."

Lily let out the breath she'd been holding. "If Rick performed the rituals, why did you take the fall for him?"

Marcia squirmed in her seat. "He promised he would help me start up my own business if I went along with this plan."

Lily's mind went into overdrive. Why would she ever believe Marcia was capable of burning bodies? She shouldn't have taken that at face value. She knew better. "He promised to help you start your own business? What kind of business?"

"We were going to start up our own funeral home. That way I could manage the make-up application and he could still do his rituals."

Lily frowned. To think those two were going to take money from people who believed their loved ones were getting the services they requested but instead were being sacrificed in a fake ritual to make money. Her stomach ached. Anger bubbled up. "That's exactly what I wanted to hear."

Marcia looked down at her hands. "I'm sorry to disappoint you. I know you think I can be saved but it's not true. I'm corrupted."

Lily sighed. She couldn't help feeling maternal towards Marcia. There had to be something to redeem her. "Do you even see that what you've done is wrong? Or have I wasted my time trying to get you on the right side?"

"I know what I did was wrong, but I wanted something different in my life. I thought Rick could give that to me. He seemed like my ticket to another life."

"He is your ticket to another life, jail life." Lily's voice came out irritated. But she took a minute to calm herself. She had more questions and a willing participant. "If Rick performed the rituals, what was your role in it?"

"I helped procure the bodies and I developed the pamphlets that were given out to prospective followers."

"So you made those. How industrious of him to use your skills for evil."

Marcia didn't respond.

Lily needed to curb her anger and try something else. "Marcia, did you really believe in his mission?" She cocked her head to the side. Saying those words felt odd. Even though cults are a reality in the world, it was hard to put herself in Marcia's position.

"I believed in his passion and commitment. I thought he was the answer to my problems."

"And then he turned into your worst nightmare."

"Seems so."

"Shortcuts don't pay off. Hard work does. If you wanted to open a funeral home, there were other more legal ways to do that. It's a shame because you are so talented."

"I told you I'm messed up."

She could hear Marcia's voice crack. And then she heard familiar footsteps approaching. James had come to check on her.

"Did you hear anything?" Lily asked him.

"I heard enough to know that Marcia was not the one wearing the black T-shirt. Interesting discovery, detective—I mean, ma'am. You don't want to be a detective anymore but you're so good at it."

"Can't argue with you."

James glanced at Marcia. "I hate to call off the party, but we have the victims' families here. We'll need to explain what happened to them."

"Can't wait." Lily gave Marcia one more look and then turned away. There was nothing more to say. She'd done all she could to find the good in Marcia. Only time would tell.

Chapter Twenty-Five

With James following close behind her, Lily walked into the conference room where the family of Ms. Linda Bernardo and Mr. Klaus Gusev sat opposite each other across a small table. Katia Gusev squeezed a tissue in her right hand while the other hand cradled her stomach. Stuart Bernardo had been Linda Bernardo's husband. His wrinkled face remained expressionless as Lily and James took their seats.

Lily kept her clammy hands on her thighs. She never had to give bad news to families. In her line of work the bad news had already been given to the family and her job was to give them peace as well as a final resting place for their loved one. But James had to deal with the bad news all the time. Another aspect of law enforcement she did not love.

"Thank you for coming. Let me first say I'm so sorry for what's taken place. The circumstances that occurred have never happened in this funeral home before and it never will happen again."

Lily watched for Stuart and Katia's expressions. Katia had been wiping away tears since she sat down while Stuart's expression remained stoic.

"What happened to my poor Klaus?" Katia said in between sniffles.

"It seems we had an infiltration into our family

business by someone who called themselves a friend."

"Oh, that's terrible," Katia remarked. "What a betrayal."

"That's exactly right. It was completely unexpected. We were blind-sided."

James cleared his throat and added. "But luckily, Lily had some suspicions and she pursued him until she could prove his guilt."

"Unfortunately, I couldn't get to him fast enough," Lily added.

James stood and walked around the table to give Lily's shoulders a squeeze. She swallowed. Her heart sank to her knees. She'd been ruthless in getting Rick to pay the piper, but it hadn't been fast enough for these families.

"Rick Drakon came to Manorview with a plan. He'd been invited to stay here to help us out. Since he was a detective, we thought he would be an asset to us."

"A detective?" Stuart Bernardo blurted out. "So you had a crooked cop?"

"It appears so."

"That's a pretty good cover."

Lily nodded at him. "It's a very good one. Until he began behaving suspiciously and infiltrating my staff. Eventually, I found out what he was doing with my clients."

Katia's eyes went wide. She gripped the tissue to her chest.

Lily continued. "Rick Drakon was a con artist. All he wanted was to be seen as powerful and cunning. He tricked many people out of their hard-earned cash. He decided my funeral home would be perfect for his next scheme."

Stuart leaned forward while his knee bounced up and down. "What did he do with the bodies?"

Rhythmic thundering in Lily's chest made her want to faint. She took in several deep breaths. "The evidence suggests that he burned them in a ritualistic type of sacrifice."

Katia cried out first. James moved in close to console her. "My poor Klaus. How could this happen?"

Stuart rubbed his eyes. "What kind of evil person would do this?"

"Someone who didn't care about anyone but himself. Someone who was raised in an atmosphere of criminal behavior," Lily replied.

The veins in Stuart's neck visibly pulsed. "Why would he do that? That sounds like something an insane person would do."

"It is insane. He was charging people money to be part of the ritual while he exalted himself as their leader. He was basically running a cult."

Stuart shook his head. "This is unbelievable."

Lily turned to face Katia. "I want you to know we would not have caught him without your help."

Katia looked up from her tissue.

"The list of names you gave me is what led us down the right path."

Katia cracked a small smile. "That was Klaus working through me. He would never want this guy to go unpunished. He wanted me to give you the list."

Lily smiled in return. "I believe it. This was a terrible tragedy."

Katia sniffed. "At least no one else was affected." She smiled. "I like the idea that Klaus had one more task to perform in this world. It suits his personality. Now he can rest in peace."

James chuckled. "That's one way to look at it. He was a brave soul."

"Indeed," Katia replied.

Stuart pursued his lips and looked at James. "You say Rick was a friend? How can you have missed this behavior? You're a detective, are you not?"

James nodded. "Fair enough. We weren't that close. He lived in The City, so we didn't see each other all that often."

Stuart's eyebrows went up.

James slapped his thigh. "In full disclosure I may not have wanted to believe he was doing those things. I met Rick when we both worked at NYPD. He was introduced to me as the schmoozer because he had a way of getting people to like him. It worked on me. I liked him. There was no reason to suspect anything. Whatever he was doing behind everyone's back he was getting away with right under everyone's nose."

"He never said anything about wanting easy money?" Lily asked. "Or was it the power he loved?"

"What man doesn't want more money or more clout? His upbringing wasn't great."

Lily's ears perked up. "Wasn't great?"

"I don't know the details, but I know his parents exposed him to crime as a child. I assumed that's why he went the other way into law enforcement to try and stay away from trouble"

"Sick people." Katia added.

James looked at Lily. "I'm the last person who would judge someone's past."

"You're a detective. Isn't that what you're supposed to do?" Stuart asked.

James slumped in his chair, looking defeated. "You're right. Maybe I should retire."

Lily turned to him. "You are good. But you were blinded by your friendship."

"I'm sorry for both of you," James said to Katia and Stuart.

"I'd like to have a small memorial for Linda and Klaus here if you'd allow it, a gathering to remember them," Lily said.

"That sounds lovely," Katia replied.

Stuart nodded. "Yes, that would be nice."

"Perfect. Thank you for coming and being so understanding."

Katia and Stuart stood up and made their way to the front door as Lily hoped they had renewed confidence in her and the Reynolds Funeral Home. Katia's tears seemed to have dried up for the moment. Lily took that as a positive sign.

"Thanks for coming," she said as the two walked to their cars. "We'll talk soon." She waved and hated the awkwardness in the setting of overwhelming guilt.

"I think that went well," James said.

"It went as well as this horrible mess could have but it's incredibly embarrassing."

He shut the door after she walked back inside. "It's over. We can move on to the next embarrassing thing."

Lily turned and shot him the death stare.

"Oh, come on. You're now going to host weddings here. From experience I know they're nothing but trouble."

She cocked her head. "We'll see about that."

"And now you have to plan a memorial for Klaus and Linda. I'm sure there won't be anything awkward about that."

Lily chuckled. "It gets worse." She led him into her office and closed the door.

James sat in one of the chairs. "How so?"

Lily made her way to her seat behind her desk. "Marcia admitted that it was Rick who slashed my tires." She gave him an I-told-you-so smirk.

James bowed. "I stand corrected."

"There's more."

"I don't think I can stand *more*."

Her smile faded. "Antonio was in on it, too."

"No."

Lily nodded. "Rick paid him to transport the bodies out of here without detection."

James covered his face with his hands. "Wow. I wasn't expecting that."

"I wasn't expecting *any* of it."

"We need to do a better job hiring."

Lily slapped the table. "I mean, who could possibly predict this?"

"Does he know we know?"

"Chris said he hasn't come to work for the last two days, and Zachary has been covering for him. Antonio was either tipped off or started feeling the heat."

James rubbed his eyes. "I'll have to bring him in."

Lily sat back in her chair, exhausted from the day. Having to explain why your business lost bodies to someone like Rick was terrible enough but losing good employees to the same person had infuriated her. "Will it finally be over then?"

"I wish I had a crystal ball to know for certain but since I don't, keep your eyes peeled."

Lily sighed. "Sure thing, detective."

Chapter Twenty-Six

Lily opened a window in the viewing room of her funeral home to let in the unseasonably warm air. Dense fog hung over the neighborhood like an unwelcome blanket. She had set up the room for a small gathering to honor the lives of Klaus Gusev and Linda Bernardo. And when she finished, a sense of calm had come over her in the process, as if this was the closure that she and everyone else involved needed.

"You did a nice job," James said, approaching her in a crisp black suit. She'd given him the bright blue paisley tie for his birthday last winter. The way the blue brought out his eyes made her giddy.

"Thanks. Did you know Zachary is bringing Julie?"

James made his way to the buffet table. "Are they back together? I had no idea."

"I guess they are. That was Rick's doing."

James looked up from the platter of grilled shrimp. "*He* got them back together? Wow. I guess he did something good." He popped a shrimp in his mouth.

"Hey, don't start eating yet. The guests of honor haven't even arrived and keep your voice down. You don't want them to hear you complimenting Rick Drakon."

"What about Rick Drakon?" Zachary announced as he walked in the room with Julie close behind him.

"Ah, speak of the devil," James said, slapping Zachary's back. "Hey, Julie."

Lily shook her head. "Nothing. There's nothing to say about Rick. But we're glad you're both here."

"It's good to see you," Julie said, as she hugged Lily.

"Julie? Is that you?" Shanna's voice rang out.

Julie laughed as she turned to Shanna's open arms. "It's me."

"Good to see you," Shanna said, rubbing Julie's back in between squeezes.

Lily fluttered around the room making sure everything looked perfect as Stuart Bernardo and Katia Gusev made their way inside.

"This is lovely," Katia said, looking around at the white lilies and blush roses spread throughout the room.

"Come in, come in. We have some small dishes if you're hungry," Lily said, gesturing toward the buffet.

"Oh, I'm too nervous to eat," Katia said.

"I'm not," Stuart said barreling his way to the platter filled with pigs-in-a-blanket.

Lily came up to Katia. "There's nothing to be nervous about. We're here as friends." Lily walked her to a seat in front of the photomontage display of Klaus and Linda.

Shanna—God bless her—sat next to Katia to keep her company.

"No Abrams?" Lily asked, noticing she'd come solo.

"You know him, always doing the most while looking like he's doing the least."

"That's an interesting way of putting it."

Shanna continued. "He promised to stop by after he wrestled with the mountain of paperwork on his desk."

"His words I take it?"

Shanna nodded. "Exactly."

"Well, he's the one missing out on a rockin' good time. His loss."

Shanna chuckled. "Agreed. I promise to give him a hard time later."

"Deal."

Lily looked around at their small gathering. Her staff had dwindled to bare bones but at least she had no anxiety about who was in the room. She noticed her manager, Chris Tuchman enter the room as she walked toward the front. She nodded at him as he sat in the audience near Zachary. With Marcia and Antonio officially off the payroll, Chris didn't have many people to manage. She'd have to consider new hires fast before he got bored and left them as well.

"Good afternoon, everyone. Thank you for coming. I thought spending the day honoring and remembering those we've lost would help with the healing we all need after the tragedy we've had to endure." Lily gestured toward Stuart and Katia. "No one suffered more than the families. I can thankfully say that the threat is no longer with us and we can now lay our client's family members to rest in peace."

A rumble of acknowledgement and light clapping ensued.

"Peace? What a luxury. To have peace in one's life," a deep raspy voice rang out from the entrance.

Lily turned around to face the intruder. As the figure slowly emerged from the shadows, her stomach sank to her knees as she realized he had a gun in his hand. and it was pointed at her.

"Antonio?" Lily asked, her knees buckled, almost

sending her to the ground. But she remained upright in the same position at the front of the room. His dark eyes stared straight into hers. Anger made his upper lip quiver. Lily heard rustling from the group behind her. No doubt James wanted to make a move.

"Don't move," he barked, waving his gun at anyone who looked threatening to him. "I have no problem shooting all of you."

Lily watched his disheveled brown hair fall into his eyes as he waved the gun around. Of course he was upset. They had spoiled his plans.

"Now what am I supposed to do?" Antonio snarled. His bloodshot eyes gave him a crazed look. This was not a crazed man. This was a desperate man.

"Antonio, it's all right." She put her hands up in defense. "We can work out a deal."

"Deal?" He pointed the gun straight at her. "There's no deal. I have no future now."

James had a gun with him. She could only imagine the amount of frustration he must be going through at this moment. If only she had access to her gun but why would she carry one to a memorial gathering?

"Antonio," James announced. "I'm not sure you've thought this through. What were you planning to do here? Shoot everyone?"

An audible gasp came from Katia.

Antonio shifted his attention to James. He'd stopped pointing the gun at Lily.

She turned her neck to see that James had stood and was clearly trying to take the attention off her.

"Yeah, Antonio." Zachary stood up. "You were really going to shoot me after all we've been through?"

The gun swung over to point at Zachary. Antonio

gritted his teeth. Sweat pooled above his brow. There were too many people for him to round up.

Lily saw the look in James's eyes. Fear mixed with determination. Her limbs began to tingle as her own fears rose to the surface. Things were happening too fast to think straight.

She watched James snatch his gun out of its holster. As soon as he did Antonio swung his gun back over to James. Shots rang out from all sides. Screams from the crowd added to the noise and commotion. Lily ducked down to the ground, hoping against all odds that no one had any target skills.

A moment of quiet went by before Lily popped up from the floor to look for James. Their eyes met as her heart thumped in terror. He stayed on the ground as she ran to his side. Blood stained the black fabric over his left shoulder. Lily searched for more wounds but didn't find any. She took her cardigan off and pushed down on his wound. He grimaced and sucked in a breath.

"Are you alright?" She asked, already knowing the answer. Thankfully, she could hear Chris calling for an ambulance. She knew she could count on him.

"I'm fine, just a little bruise." He groaned and closed his eyes. "Better me than you."

"You would say that."

It dawned on her that she was going through the same scenario that he did when his ex-girlfriend, Andrea, died in a crossfire. He took the bullet this time instead of going through the agony of losing someone again. Except this time Lily wouldn't let him die. She forced back the tears and grabbed his face with her free hand. "You stay with me. You got that."

He chuckled and then scrunched up his face. "I'm

too scared of you to die."

"Good." But the truth was she didn't know. She didn't know if the bullet hit a major artery and if he had only a few minutes left with her. "And don't forget, I love you."

He opened his eyes and smiled. The blue in his eyes was as bright as the sky. He cleared his throat and said in a whisper. "I love you, too."

Finally, the paramedics came bursting into the room to attend to the wounded. She backed away to let them get him on a stretcher and stabilized. She glanced at the area where Antonio had been standing. His lifeless body now lay on the floor as another set of paramedics tried to revive him. James's bullet had gone through Antonio's chest, a much more dire circumstance. She hadn't considered Antonio's fate. It hadn't mattered in the face of losing James.

Shanna rushed to her side. She buried her face in her hands. "Are you alright?"

"Nothing happened to *me*. But he could've taken down the whole room. Is anyone hurt?" Lily announced to the others.

"No, we are fine," Zachary said, holding Julie's hand.

Lily glanced at Katia and Stuart. She had just finished promising them a crime free experience in her funeral home. There was nothing she could say to make it better nor did she have the energy to try.

"Is James all right?" Zachary asked.

"I think he'll be fine. He was very lucky. I'm going with them in the ambulance. You guys stay here and keep our guests company." She turned toward her manager. "Chris, you hold down the fort."

She turned to her sister. "Shanna, call Abrams to let him know what happened."

"I already have." Shanna replied.

"The police are going to want a statement from everyone," Lily said as she rushed toward the exit but then turned around once more. "I'm so sorry this happened."

Then she sprinted toward the ambulance with James inside. Her heart leaped into her throat. She didn't want to alarm the others, but she didn't really know if he was going to make it. Antonio had not. And what would she do if he didn't? Images of her life with James flashed before her eyes.

From the moment when she'd first laid eyes on his silky black hair and tattooed biceps in the basement of her funeral home to their wedding day when he told her they would be together forever, this could not be the end. She would not want to go on. Tears flooded her eyes, clouding her vision as she ran toward the ambulance James had been loaded into. Yanking the back door open wide, she propelled herself inside.

His eyes were closed but his body had been hooked up to monitors that beeped incessantly. Intravenous fluids ran down the tubing and into James's arms. And there was blood—lots of blood on the floor of the truck and on the linens of the stretcher. She willed herself into tunnel vision to avoid seeing nothing but red. The paramedics sat on opposite sides of the ambulance monitoring the machines hooked up to him.

She stood at the foot of the stretcher watching for any movement. Was he unconscious? Had he slipped into a coma? Was he only minutes from death? She'd stopped breathing altogether until she touched his leg and his eyes popped open.

"You know, this is the first time I've ever been shot." His eyes sparkled with mischief.

She released the air from her lungs and chuckled at him. Her heart could beat again. "Congratulations. I'll tell you what you've won later. Now work on not dying."

He smiled and laid his head back on the pillow. "Yes, ma'am."

Chapter Twenty-Seven

"I'm thrilled neither Rick nor Antonio murdered anyone," Abrams said, raising his glass of beer for a sip.

"That is a plus. Although it was close." James nodded in his direction. "But that might've made this wedding slightly less expensive with fewer guests to invite."

Lily smacked his good shoulder. "That's far too gruesome to say at my sister's wedding."

"We are at a funeral home. I don't think anything is off limits," James replied. "And watch the shoulder smacks. I'm already down one."

Lily petted his right arm. "I know I'm too rough."

"And what a beautiful job Lily has done," Gina Giordani said from across the table. She'd brought a mystery man Lily had never seen before.

The gray near his temple and solid fit physique gave him a distinctive look. She couldn't help but wonder if he might be an ex-gang member or a criminal since he was hanging around Gina. It was hard to tell. Going by his stoic expression he was not someone Lily should mess with.

"Former FBI special agent, Charlie Mesa," James whispered in her ear. "Quite the legend in his day."

Lily nodded, then turned to Gina. "This house does it all by itself. All I did was call a few people to bring food and drinks. The real test will be in a couple of weeks when I have our first client wedding."

She wondered if Charlie had been the guy Gina called for inside information on Rick. It would make sense. The idea set Lily's mind into a tailspin. Had Charlie known about the case? Had he been tracking Rick? Lily knew the FBI wouldn't normally follow this type of case but had Rick been on Charlie's radar for other reasons?

Gina looked around. "Based on what you've accomplished here I'm certain your client will be more than happy."

Lily smiled in return. She admired the punk rock meets wedding chic look Gina had come up with today. Her blonde hair had been slicked back on the sides while the top had been combed into a fauxhawk. Black kohl lined her lower lids, but her satin lavender strapless dress softened the whole look.

"I have to be honest with you, Lily," Abrams said, pulling her out of her thoughts, "I wasn't sure about this place for a wedding, but it works. Did I hear correctly that you're also opening it up for weddings for hire on the side."

"That's right, Don, I'm always thinking ahead."

"Maybe you could do Halloween parties, too. It's got that creepy vibe."

"All right, I think you've gone too far, boss," James scolded. "I think you're a little scared you just tied the knot against your own self-professed principles."

"Oh!" Zachary burst out laughing while Julie grabbed his arm to shush him.

Abrams looked at James. "You want to go for round two? I owe you a right hook."

"Nah, you've been drinking. The fight will end the

same way even with my bum shoulder—with you on the ground."

Abrams smirked at him. "I might not be as young and fast as you, but you've got a hell of a lot more baggage." He sipped his beer.

James scrunched up his face. "Is that right?"

Abrams nodded. "Mm-hmm. But you don't have to worry. I'm not going to treat you any differently even though I know what happened in your past about Andrea."

James swallowed hard to prevent from spitting out his drink. "You do? Who told you?"

"Shanna told me. Put it this way, I get why you act the way you do toward Lily, so protective all the time."

James rolled his eyes. "Wonderful. Are you going to walk on eggshells around me now?"

"Are you kidding? If anything I have more dirt now to make fun of you."

"Hey," Shanna said as she shimmied over to the table in her glittering white dress, "stop the fussing. Let's go dance. I'd rather you make a fool of yourself on the dance floor. Come on, husband."

"You heard the lady," James added.

"Fine." Abrams guzzled the last of his drink. "At least we know no one is sneaking around the place looking to steal a body or two. Lily, for that I am thankful." He raised his glass toward her while his other hand was being pulled by Shanna. He had no choice but to get up and go with her.

Lily noticed Charlie Mesa perked up at Abrams's last comment. She wanted to know why. Sliding her chair toward Gina, she knew James would understand.

"I can't tell you how integral you were in helping us

with Rick," she said to Gina. "If you hadn't given us the information about the cemeteries, we'd probably be missing more bodies." Lily noticed Charlie had leaned forward to listen.

"It's no trouble. This is my friend Charlie." Gina leaned out of the way to introduce him to Lily.

"Nice to meet you." Lily shook his hand. He held her hand in a firm grip before letting go.

"Are you the famous sleuth Gina's been telling me about?" Charles asked in a voice that thundered as opposed to simply stating. "Better be careful, it's ugly out there."

"You wouldn't be the first to give out that advice." That's all she needed, another overprotective presence in her life.

"Especially with people like Rick Drakon. The FBI has been tracking him for a while. He's been involved in funeral home scams for some time. When he skipped town and landed here, they didn't know where he was headed."

Lily's eyes went wide. "That's insane."

"When people would still hire him, his last scam involved selling body parts and putting concrete powder in people's urns to fake the ashes. It's taken some time to put all the pieces together."

Lily's hand covered her mouth in shock. "How could he do that and still be a detective?"

"He isn't a detective now despite what he's been telling people."

Lily's jaw dropped. "He's a completely different person, leading a double life."

Charlie nodded. "It appears so. He walked away from law enforcement when they started asking him too many questions."

She thought about how James might feel hearing this—he'd be devastated. All that trust and confidence in someone had been a waste of his time.

Charles continued. "When Gina called, I knew we had something, thanks to you."

"I believed going to her would help but I had no idea you would be on the other line."

"What did you think?" Gina smirked. "That I had some mafia contact on the other line?"

Lily's cheeks flushed. "I wasn't sure. You're very…private."

Gina chuckled. "Are you admitting to believing everything you hear?"

"No." Lily's hand went up against her chest. "But I have to say this is a surprise." Lily glanced at James who had been watching her the entire time. "I wanted to get to know you better, but I didn't think you'd be open to sharing."

"I'm somewhat open. I think we have more in common than I previously thought. You're quite a gangster in your own way."

"Which brings me to my next question." Lily smiled, feeling a bit awkward. "James thought since we lost Marcia maybe you could come be our make-up artist."

Gina laughed—a rare sight. "I'm flattered but I love my shop and I'm not sure I could handle both."

Lily wondered if Gina and Charles were dating. Physically, they looked good together, but her checkered past seemed at odds with his straight edge lifestyle. Or maybe crime was something they have in common. She was no dating expert. "At least consider working for us on a part-time basis. I think you'd be great."

Gina smiled. "I will."

Lily felt James come up next to her. His hand went out. "A dance, my lady."

She smiled looking up at him. "Certainly." She took his hand as he led her to the dance floor.

"I waited." He said as he led them to a less crowded spot on the dance floor.

"For what?"

"A slow song," he said, pulling her against him. "It took ages."

She put her arms around his neck careful not to disturb his shoulder. Even though he'd mostly recovered, the long road of surgery to fix the bones, and physical therapy, had been extensive.

"What'd you learn?" he asked.

"Too many things." She shook her head. "The gist is that Rick wasn't who you thought he was for longer than you thought."

"I could guess that based on the level of crazy. Anything else?"

"Is that why you didn't want to believe me for so long? Maybe you didn't want to know?"

"Maybe. I also hated the idea that I'm the one who invited him into our lives. That makes it my fault."

"How would you have known? Plus, I get to be right again, which you know I enjoy."

"I know. What did Charlie and Gina have to say?"

"Charlie confirmed Rick's long history of scams and Gina politely declined our offer to hire her. Although, I'll keep trying."

He stared down into her eyes as they turned to the music. "How are you feeling about Antonio?"

She sighed. "I'm shocked and disappointed. Granted, the only staff I really trusted was family and now I know why my parents chose to keep it that way. How about you? You were the one he shot."

"You have said that I'm the one blinded by my friendship with Rick. Antonio was not on your radar because you trusted him, remember."

"True. But in the end that was Rick's fault again. If he hadn't approached Antonio with an offer he couldn't refuse, Antonio would still be alive. Rick brainwashed everyone."

"You did a great job identifying Rick. Are you sure you won't consider re-joining the force?"

"I consider myself part of the team but I'm not switching careers. I'll have to check my ego...sometimes."

James smirked. "Will you slap me if I agree with that statement?"

"I'm shocked you had to ask. I know this sounds like good news to you—less danger and all but I think it's a good compromise."

"Agreed. Unless you want to ditch the entire sleuthing thing all together which would help me sleep better at night?"

"No chance. You sleep fine."

James's eyes sparkled with mischief as he swung Lily around and used his good shoulder to lean her into a dip. "That's because you sleep right next to me."

She smiled as he went in for a quick soft kiss and then slowly pulled away, leaving her stomach aflutter. "How did I get so lucky?"

A word about the author...

When Ana Diamond isn't writing about tough gals finding love in unexpected places, she's at work by day in the medical field. She writes cozy romantic mystery novels with feisty strong women and alluring men who can't resist them. Her books are fast paced, entertaining and heartfelt all at once.

Ana is a 2020 Tara Contest Finalist for Body Conscious and 2015 Melody of Love contest finalist. She lives in New York with her husband and two children.

http://anadiamondauthor.com